PRAISE FOR
KRISTINE KATHRYN RUSCH

"Rusch is a great storyteller."

—*RT Book Reviews*

"Whether [Rusch] writes high fantasy, horror, sf, or contemporary fantasy, I've always been fascinated by her ability to tell a story with that enviable gift of invisible prose. She's one of those very few writers whose style takes me right into the story—the words and pages disappear as the characters and their story swallows me whole....Rusch has style."

—Charles de Lint

"A masterful writer is at work."

—Orson Scott Card

"Rusch's greatest strength...is her ability to close down a story and leave the reader feeling that the author could not possibly have wrung any more satisfaction out of the piece."

—*The Kansas City Star*

"Rusch is a great storyteller—easily the equal of Patterson or Koontz."

—*Analog*

"Kristine Kathryn Rusch is one of the best writers in the field."

—*SFRevu*

"[Rusch's] writing style is simple but elegant, and her characterization excellent."

—Mark Morris
Beyond

"Kristine Kathryn Rusch's crime stories are exceptional, both in plot and in style."

—Ed Gorman
Mystery Scene Magazines

Praise for the Fey series

"Rusch writes with a transparent, impeccable readable grace ... suprising and original ... Rusch makes daring authorial choices here as she crafts something much more complex than merely an epic about war."

—*Sword and Sorcery*
on *The Fey: Changeling*

"A very good, very large fantasy ... nicely done and with a particularly satisfying and unexpected resolution."

—*Science Fiction Chronicle*
on *The Fey: Sacrifice*

Also by
Kristine Kathryn Rusch

The Retrieval Artist Series:

The Fey Series:

Five Feline Fancies
Kristine Kathryn Rusch

wMG
Publishing

Five Feline Fancies

"The Secret Lives of Cats" by Kristine Kathryn Rusch was first published in Ellery Queen's Mystery Magazine, July, 2008.

"Scrawny Pete" by Kristine Kathryn Rusch was first published as an Amazon Short, June, 2005.

"What Fluffy Knew" by Kristine Kathryn Rusch was first published in Alien Pets, edited by Denise Little, Daw Books, 1998.

"The Poop Thief" by Kristine Kathryn Rusch was first published in Enchantment Place, edited by Denise Little, Daw Books, 2008.

"Destiny" by Kristine Kathryn Rusch was first published in French as "Destin" in Faeries: Toutes Les Fantasy, Hiver 2000-2001; and first published in English in Creature Fantastic, edited by Denise Little, Daw Books, 2001.

WMG Publishing
www.wmgpublishing.com

Contents

Five Feline Fancies
Kristine Kathryn Rusch

Introduction

MAYBE I WRITE ABOUT CATS because I live with them. I have had as many as 12 and as few as one. Much as I love them, I do feel as if I'm living with alien creatures. I understand what they do, but the understanding is shallow. I can predict their behavior, but never truly know why they do what they do.

The only cats in this collection who are pure cats are the cats in "The Secret Lives of Cats." Inspired by a German photographer who really did rig up cameras on his outdoor cats, I thought as I read about him what if his cats brought home pictures of an unexpected subject?

Sometimes I think Solanda, the Fey Shapeshifter whose chosen form is feline, is also a true cat. She's loyal, but surprised by it. Her story spreads through the first few novels of the Fey. "Destiny" happens before those dark days.

I wrote "What Fluffy Knew" and "The Poop Thief" for invitation anthologies on particular subjects. I wrote "Fluffy" for *Alien Pets*. Since I already thought cats were alien, I decided to explore something else. That thought, along with the recent death of my very pampered cat Ashley, inspired "Fluffy."

I wrote "The Poop Thief" for an anthology called *Enchantment Place*, a loosely collected group of magic-shop stories. I had no idea at all for the anthology until I heard an ad for a local clean-up company that promised to "steal the poop from your backyard." Suddenly, in the rather magical ways that stories come about, I had "The Poop Thief."

As for "Scrawny Pete," I have no idea where that story came from. It just happened one day. Rather like Scrawny Pete himself, I think.

Anyway, I hope you enjoy this small group of stories. I will publish other five story collections. They'll unify around genre or topic. So enjoy this first offering. I had fun putting it together.

—Kristine Kathryn Rusch
Lincoln City, Oregon
July 1, 2010

The Secret Lives of Cats

*H*OMER ZIFF didn't believe in old adages, but after his long and eventful spring, he couldn't help but think that whoever put the words "curiosity," "cat," and "kill" in the same sentence had to be onto something.

It all began about his own curiosity—about his cats. Homer Ziff lived alone with two indoor cats and six outdoor cats. Well, six he could pet and hold; there were others—the friends, neighbors and hangers-on, he called them—who visited at meal time or for a rest on the back forty in the mid-afternoon sun.

Not that he had a real back forty. But his back yard was an impressive three acres, complete with woods and stream. One of the reasons he bought the house was that it had the best of both worlds: in the front, he had a small lawn that led to a quiet residential street; in the back, he had the acres of property that covered a protected wetland. No one would ever build behind him, the lots next to him were full, and the houses across the street had reached their maximum size according to code.

He knew his neighbors by sight (rather like he knew their cats) and he would nod at them whenever he saw them, but didn't engage in conversation. He couldn't bring himself to talk to them, not after his first attempt, when he'd stuttered at a man several doors down, and the man had rolled his eyes and walked away.

Homer would liked to have blamed his surly neighbor for his own lack of congeniality, but that wouldn't be fair or accurate. Homer didn't engage most people in conversation. He had a stutter that got worse when he was nervous.

Over the years, he'd learned to prefer his own company. He liked being alone with his thoughts and his cats and his property.

And it was his thoughts that made being alone possible. Not that his thoughts were original—sadly, they weren't—but they were organized, and that had given him an edge. Once upon a time, he had been a professor of physics at Oregon State University. A rising star when he was hired, he'd become a stalled star by mid-career— a man for whom the great things expected never materialized.

Which would have been well and good except that stalled stars had to be stellar teachers and he was not. He was pathologically shy, and his stutter got worse in front of large groups. He was better one on one, but stalled stars weren't allowed to teach the smaller classes. He had to teach some large sections as well, and he dreaded them like he dreaded a visit to the dentist.

But he did have one valuable skill. He could explain things clearly. His gift of clarity had gotten him through graduate school and into an important teaching position, but that gift also stalled him. And it made him into something of a rebel.

Because of his gift, he threw out the suggested text for 101 Physics (a more confusing book he'd never seen) and wrote a series of notes that sold in the campus bookstore—not just to his students, but to students from other physics classes. The bookstore owner called him one day to ask whether students at the nearby University of Oregon could purchase the notes. Then students from some of the private colleges made the drive from McMinnville and Portland to get his notes, and finally, the chairman of his department said, "Y'know, Ziff, you could make a fortune on those notes if you just turned them into a book."

So he did. It became the number one 101 physics text in the country, which led his publisher to ask if he would write a simple physics book for the masses, which he did, and another for children, which he did, and suddenly Homer Ziff no longer needed to worry about being a stalled star. He had become a rising star again—or maybe even an established one—and could have his pick of the course load within his department.

Only the books had given him another gift. Financial independence. He no longer had to teach. And since standing in front of students made him so nervous that he sometimes spent the hour before class in the restroom, he decided that the prudent move would be to quit.

He bought his marvelous house, made sure his finances were in order, and then retired to write a half dozen more popular science books, with more under contract.

Some days, the cats were his only companions. He didn't mind, really. He never stuttered when he spoke to cats, and they didn't care that he lacked original thought.

They were happy that he provided food and shelter and a bit of companionship.

He was happy to have them purr.

Because of them, he had become a little cat-obsessed.

He had been surfing the net one night when he discovered a website designed by a man in Germany. The man sounded like a kindred spirit. He lived with a cat to whom he devoted an inordinate amount of time. That cat was an indoor-outdoor cat, and the German man wondered how his cat spent his time outside the house.

So the man, who appeared to be some kind of engineer, modified a digital camera, put it around his cat's neck, set it up to take pictures every minute and a half, and sent the cat on its way. The resulting photographs were charming and inspiring.

Homer found himself staring at his outdoor friends, wondering how their days went. One cat's routine illuminated the life of one cat. Six cats' routines might actually be the beginning of some kind of scientific study.

At least, that was what he told himself as he used the

instructions on the German man's website to build six catcams. After some struggle, Homer managed to attach them to five of his outdoor favorites (he gave up on the wily old tom—who not only drew blood, but managed to slice him up badly enough to require fifteen stitches on his left hand).

Then he sent the five on their mission, hoping to discover the secret lives of cats.

***

AND HE DID. He discovered all sorts of marvelous things.

He saw the same feline faces in his yard, in his neighbor's yard, at the century-old schoolhouse down the street. He realized that each cat had not only its own routine, but shared a neighborhood routine as well.

Mornings began at his house, with a treat of kibble and soft food, followed by a trek to the dumpster behind the local Burger King, then to a long rest under the bleachers at the old school.

The ground beneath his neighbors' cars and his own Ford pick-up served as sites for daily conferences. A house three blocks away provided an afternoon snack, usually followed by a dumpster diving at a local fish market and the nearby Diary Queen.

On warm days, the cats tromped down to the wetlands for drinks from the springs that prevented anyone from building behind Homer's property.

He would have blessed those springs, if he hadn't seen something curious.

On the earliest photos the springs looked like a primeval swampland. Cats, due to their low-to-the-ground perspective, took the most amazing photographs. Apparently the wetlands at dawn (or was it dusk?) had ground fog, which made everything opaque and surreal.

The swamp (he didn't know what else to call it) had tree limbs and branches and sticks rising from the muck, all hidden by the ghost-like grayness of the fog. To his surprise, the cats didn't drink from the water here. They sat in front of it—all five of them—as if they were watching something.

Subsequent photos on different days showed something that resembled an elephant's graveyard. What he'd initially thought were tree branches were bones sticking out of the mud. Some of the bones were covered in moss. Others had ivy growing around them like large green cobwebs.

The ivy gave him some perspective, but not enough. He couldn't tell what kind of bones these were. Cats are small creatures and the cameras took photographs from that small perspective. Bones which seemed huge in some photographs seemed tiny in others.

Those others, he soon realized, were taken from some kind of height. Either that particular feline photographer had climbed a tree or it sat on a bank or it watched from a stump.

Homer found it curious that the cats never got close to the elephant's graveyard. They always sat back. But as the weeks went on and the photographs accumulated, Homer realized that the graveyard was a spring haunt, just like the school had been in the winter.

The cats weren't interested in food; they were observing something.

And that intrigued him.

Because cats, like humans, had a scientific turn of mind.

***

He had noticed that scientific frame of mind from the day he brought home his first kitten. Cats not only studied things, but they made a study of things. One of his cats decided to probe the mysteries of ice cubes—how they turned into water, whether they could be carried, why they sometimes shattered. Another spent an entire week learning how the front door knob turned. Eventually that cat learned how to turn the knob herself; fortunately she never did figure out the necessity of pulling the door open.

Or maybe opening the door didn't interest her. The front door was the only one with a cut glass door knob. It refracted light. Maybe the cat had been more interested in the prisms inside the knob than in using that knob to go outside.

Homer never mentioned these thoughts to anyone else. He often felt as if he put too much time into his cats. And then he discovered that German man's website, and realized he was not alone in his obsession with cat thought.

But, Homer would have wagered, the German man did not have an entire second computer devoted to the photographs that the cats created. Nor, Homer suspected, did the German man spend as much time trying to figure out what his cats were thinking as they stared—not just at the elephant graveyard, but also from underneath cars or beside Dumpsters.

The cats seemed involved in a part of life that Homer had somehow missed.

***

As the spring went on, he realized the cats were studying the elephant graveyard the same way that his indoor cat had studied that doorknob. They just hadn't gotten to the touching stage yet.

He would know when they did. Daily, he got a series of photos of the back of pink tongues, lapping water from a puddle or a stream or a bowl that someone had placed outside. He would get photographs of near-dead prey wriggling out of a mouth.

But he saw nothing like that near the bones.

Only cats, watching the swampy water as if it held the secret of the universe.

***

Then, one Sunday afternoon, everything changed.

A little white female he called Mata Hari because of her attractiveness to the males (even after she was fixed) and her tendency to wander off on dangerous and secretive missions of her own brought home a defining photograph.

Every day, she sat in the same spot near the swamp. The little camera around her neck took a variation of the same photograph—a bone fragment sticking out of the primordial ooze. Sometimes the fragment was brown with mud and sometimes it looked almost white. But, over time, he realized it was the same fragment, which meant she sat in the same spot daily, studying something that she felt was important.

Only that Sunday, the fragment was covered by a human hand.

The hand loomed in the photograph, the fingers dominating the scene. They rose upward toward the sky, the ridges of the knuckles visible against the blackness of the muck. Dried cuts marred the flesh along the back, and the fingernails—clipped short—had dirt embedded all the way down to the skin.

Mata Hari had brought home ten pictures of the hand, which meant she spent fifteen minutes contemplating it, twice as long as she usually spent at that spot. The cat had managed to get several different angles, and oddly, each was farther away than the previous one.

The hand put the other bones in perspective. He returned to his photo files, opened the relevant pictures next to the photo of the hand and compared.

His breath caught. What had seemed like animal bones—small and fragile, old, abandoned, like elephants in their graveyard—were not. They were too large. He had been more accurate with the foggy photos when he'd thought of the bones as branches and logs.

These bones were large. No domesticated animal, except maybe a Husky or a Rotweiller, would have bones like that. Nor would most of the wild animals around here. This area was too populated for bears, even with the wetlands below. Maybe a deer or two had died down there, but certainly not a bunch of them. The coyotes were the size of raccoons, and barely larger than the cats, and there were no wolves here.

Which left only one other creature that could have provided the bones.

Humans.

And the latest victim had just arrived.

***

HE NEEDED TO KNOW if any of the other cats had photographs of the hand.

He got up and peered out his window. Two of the other cats had returned. He stepped outside and removed the memory card from both cameras, careful to put in a new card before he shut the cameras off. He'd tried night photos before, but the flash had scared the cat so badly that it had run in circles, screaming.

He hadn't known cats could scream.

He gave each cat some pets and a small treat, then went back inside and downloaded the photographs.

In every bunch, a handful were duds—blurs, unrecognizable objects, a paw in front of the lens. These two batches were no different. But he set aside the blurs and unrecognizable objects this time, deciding they might be useful.

Then he scanned the images until he got to the swamp.

These cats had come to the graveyard as well, and at about the same time as Mata Hari. In fact, one of the unrecognizable objects might have been her haunch as the other cat sniffed her in greeting.

These cats stayed even farther away. He found photographs of an entire arm, covered in bruises, and a bit of shoulder. His hands were shaking as he magnified the images.

The arm and hand had clearly come from the same place. He could see the bone fragment, the moss-covered bones, the ivy-covered bones and the brackish water. Now he knew why the cats didn't drink here.

He wasn't even sure why they came—they were well fed, so they didn't need to eat decaying flesh. Were they watching something decompose? Or were they hunting the rats or some other creature that frequented the wetlands?

For the first time since he started this experiment, he felt frustrated that he couldn't ask.

And then he found the money shot.

Or what would have been a money shot had he been a photographer along the lines of Weegee—the man who photographed corpses at crime scenes.

This shot was worthy of Weegee as well: a naked woman, her back arched, arms and legs splayed over what he had once thought were branches, her face turned toward the camera.

His shaking grew worse as he magnified this image. Her face had no real expression. The mouth was open, battered and bloody, the nose flattened, the cheeks covered in either blood or dirt.

But the eyes got to him. The eyes didn't look human. They looked like something out of a bad horror movie—filmed over with white, unfocused, and empty. It wasn't even fair to say that they were staring, because they weren't. There was no intelligence behind them, no thought, no anything. No staring happened because there was no intelligence inside those eyes to stare.

He leaned away from the computer and frowned. Something about the image was familiar. At first he thought it was simply the way the woman had fallen, and then he realized what it was.

She had come to his door. Four days ago. She'd parked her SUV against the curb, the windows open, her daughter—who was ten, maybe eleven—crying inside.

The woman had knocked, and he almost didn't answer because she looked so angry. But when he pulled the door open, she smiled at him.

"My daughter is selling candy so that her band can go to the regional tournaments." She opened the box. "Would you like to buy something?"

He didn't look at the candy. He looked at the crying girl in the SUV, wondering what her story was. He could probably guess. She didn't want to sell the candy, but her mother tried to force her. And when that hadn't worked, the mother decided to do it herself.

"She's shy," her mother said, as if confirming his thoughts.

He couldn't condone this kind of behavior, not from an adult. He hated bullying in all its forms, having been a victim of it when he was young and skinny and too nerdy for his own good.

But the woman made him nervous, and he couldn't say what he wanted to, which was, *Let your daughter be herself. Not everyone is a good salesperson.* Or good with people. Or even good one-on-one.

Instead, he struggled with, "N-N-No th-th-thanks."

And shut the door.

The woman remained on the porch for a moment, as if she couldn't believe he'd been that rude, and then she'd walked back to the SUV. She'd tossed the box of candy at her poor daughter before getting inside, and driving away.

If she was here, in this swamp, somewhere in the neighborhood, where was the little girl?

He was reaching for the phone before he even realized what he was doing, and dialed 911. When the operator answered, he said, "I think there's a dead body in my neighborhood."

And that brought the detectives to his door.

***

THEY WERE IN plain clothes, but they showed him badges. He recognized both detectives from the local paper.

They had been working on some kind of task force, and they had their pictures in the Metro section often enough that he could almost remember their names.

Fortunately for him, he didn't need to. They introduced themselves.

The man with the silver hair trimmed so close to his neck that it looked like whiskers was Detective DeCarovich. His partner, a woman who looked like she could bench-press Homer without any effort, was Detective Ortiz.

They came inside Homer's house without invitation, and wanted to know where he had seen the body. He brought them the photograph which he'd printed out on his laser printer, and they asked again where he had seen her.

So he had to explain—slowly because his stutter acted up—about the cat cameras and the experiment. The detectives stared at him as if he were crazy, so he finally waved them over to the computer and showed them the German man's home page, complete with instructions on how to build the camera.

Ortiz was the one who finally realized that Homer was serious. She turned to him, her dark eyes wide and stunned. "You did this with your own cats?"

Then she turned toward Princess, his pampered white Persian who looked like she had starred in the Fancy Feast commercials. Princess was lying on top of the red satin pillow he had placed on his couch as a joke, and she looked about as indolent as a cat could get.

"Not her," he said. "The outdoor cats. The more or less feral ones."

DeCarovich crossed his arms. He clearly didn't believe Homer and might even think Homer had something to do with the woman's disappearance.

Homer crooked a finger. "Come with me," he said. "But quietly."

He led them into the kitchen which overlooked the back forty. Fortunately, Mata Hari was in her afternoon spot, on top of a rock near an overgrown rhododendron, stretched out and sound asleep.

"See that box around her neck?" he said. "It has her camera. There are four other cats with cameras as well."

"For godsake," DeCarovich said and shook his head. He clearly wasn't impressed. He acted more like a man who had thought he'd seen it all, only to be surprised by something this weird. "Why would you do that?"

"Curiosity," Homer said. "I wondered what they do all day."

"Eat and sleep," Ortiz said.

"Actually, no," Homer said. "They're quite active…"

And then he let his voice trail off. The detectives weren't interested in his cats. They were interested in the photographs. DeCarovich was looking at the dead woman again.

"You really don't know where this is," DeCarovich said.

"No," Homer said. "And I'm not even sure it's on my property. It could be anywhere in the neighborhood."

"Or farther," Ortiz said. "Cats can have a territory of twenty acres or more."

DeCarovich turned toward her as if she had suddenly gone as crazy as Homer.

She shrugged. "I grew up around cats."

DeCarovich let out a small laugh, the kind a person used when he discovered he was among people he thought beneath him. Homer had heard that laugh a lot as a kid, and he didn't miss it.

His face heated, and his throat tightened. The stutter would get even worse. He knew the symptoms. He had to struggle just to start his next sentence, but he knew the tricks: don't get stuck on one word. Instead, recast your sentence into something else.

"M-M-Maybe I can reconstruct where they go," he said. He led the detectives back into his study so that he could open the computer photo files. "I have d-d-days worth of photos. Maybe th-th-there are l-l-landmarks."

He called up the files and started with the swamp and elephant graveyard photos, working backwards through each cat's imagery file. He wished now he hadn't thrown out most of the blurred and unfocused photos. They might tell him something.

Ortiz was leaning over his shoulder as he worked. DeCarovich walked through the room, studying Homer's books and his framed awards.

"You wrote these?" he asked after a moment.

"Y-Y-Yes," Homer said.

"Science guy, huh?"

He wanted to go for a self-deprecating "kinda" but the "k" would give him trouble. He had to settle for another stammered "yes."

"I guess guys like you would do stuff like this. Experiments, huh?"

But Homer was careful not to answer that vague a question. He still had the sense DeCarovich believed he was involved in that woman's death.

"Th-Th-The p-p-pictures?"

"Yeah." DeCarovich looked at him.

Homer nodded. His throat had tightened so badly he knew he wouldn't be able to easily get out another sentence.

"Damn," Ortiz said beside him. "These cats go underneath everything."

They did too. Under leaves, between bushes, under rocks. There was no clear trail, nothing recognizable, at least to human eyes.

"You actually think this guy's onto something?" DeCarovich asked, no longer trying to hide his contempt.

"I think we finally found the bone yard," Ortiz said, and Homer was the one who shuddered.

He remembered the articles now. These detectives had just formed a task force to investigate a series of missing persons cases, all of women in their thirties who disappeared in broad daylight.

"Except we didn't find it, not yet," Ortiz was saying. "These cats can't tell us where it is and if we try to follow them, we'll make sure they never go there again."

"We'll have to do a grid search," DeCarovich said.

"And destroy a lot of physical evidence along the way." Ortiz sighed. "At least now we know what happened to Ann Kemmel."

"Th-Th-That's the woman?" Homer asked.

Ortiz nodded.

"Wh-Wh-What about her daughter?"

Both detectives stared at him as if he had just confessed. He swallowed and forced himself to tell them about the incident with the candy bars and the SUV.

"F-F-Four days ago," he said.

"That's when she disappeared," DeCarovich said. "Only her kid wasn't with her. Her kid was at home the whole time."

Homer shook his head. "I saw her. She was in th-th-the c-c-car."

"How would you know?" DeCarovich asked.

"She was c-c-crying real hard." He felt his face get even redder. "I th-th-thought her mother was b-b-being mean."

DeCarovich's eyes narrowed, but Ortiz didn't seem to notice. She turned toward him.

He raised his eyebrows. "I thought we were too easy on her."

"I can't believe she was lying," Ortiz said. "She must have seen something. I'll bet she was scared."

DeCarovich shook his head. "She was just another—."

He waved his hand at Homer, and Homer wondered what word DeCarovich left out.

"She st-st-st…" Homer couldn't say the word. He never could under stress. "She has a speech d-d-defect?"

"Like you," DeCarovich said.

Homer nodded. He had been right then. The mother had been treating her like his mother had treated him, believing that he could overcome his problems with just a little more hard work.

"She wasn't in the car," Ortiz said. "She was lying."

"Lying," Homer said slowly so that he wouldn't stutter any more, "makes a speech problem worse. Any stress, even small stress, will make the problem worse."

He got it out without a single mistake. His cheeks grew even hotter. DeCarovich frowned at him, but it was no longer the frown of the impatient. It was a frown of consideration.

"You think the kid saw something?" he asked Homer, and Homer got that sense again that DeCarovich still suspected him.

Homer's throat tightened, so he shrugged.

"I'll bet she did," Ortiz said. "We need to reinterview."

"With the photographic evidence." DeCarovich picked up the print-out. "Can we keep that?"

Homer nodded.

"She's going to be just as afraid of us as she was the last time." Ortiz sighed.

Homer knew what she was imagining. Trying to interview a child whose mouth continually betrayed her would be difficult at best.

Ortiz took the photograph from DeCarovich. "Too bad you can't put a video camera on those cats. Then we could

21

just find the body and the evidence. There's bound to be some if he's been using that spot for the past five years."

Five years. Homer started. They were investigating five years worth of disappearances. Five years of dumping dead women into a primeval swamp.

"It c-c-can't be t-t-too cl-cl-close," Homer said. "We'd smell it. Me and the neighbors. Bodies…"

He didn't have to finish his sentence. Ortiz was nodding.

"You're right," she said. "We need a topo map."

"You want wind charts too?" DeCarovich was being sarcastic.

"I'm serious," Ortiz said. "If we can find the body without talking to that kid—"

"We have to talk to her," DeCarovich said. "We have to know why she lied."

Homer knew DeCarovich was right. But the two thoughts—the video camera and that little girl—gave him an idea.

"D-D-Don't show her the photograph," he said. "She won't be able t-t-to t-t-talk after th-th-that."

"Listen, buddy," DeCarovich said, but Ortiz put a hand on his arm.

Homer made himself take a deep breath. "What I meant was I might b-b-be able t-t-to modify the c-c-cameras. Instead of every 90 seconds, I might be able t-t-to have images every five."

"Which just show us more leaves and trees and rocks," DeCarovich said. "Nice try, but that's going to give us more of the same."

"No," Ortiz said. "It won't. It might show us where the cats go into the woods. Can you set up a time stamp too?"

"Yes," Homer said. "If we know where they go in, the angle of the sun might tell us what direction they're going."

He realized after he spoke that he was no longer nervous. He liked the female detective. She didn't intimidate him.

"These cats aren't looking up," DeCarovich said. "We can't see sunlight."

"Through the leaves, on the ground, we'll get some stuff. C'mon, Rick," Ortiz said. "You've done similar things with shadow."

"I still think we do a grid."

"Let's give Mr. Ziff a chance," Ortiz said. "His cats might help us."

DeCarovich snorted. "Like they can do that."

"They already have," Ortiz said. "They gave us Ann Kemmel, and a reason to reinterview her daughter."

DeCarovich glared at Homer. "You get one day for this nonsense. One day. After that, we do a grid."

As if Homer had a stake in not having a grid search. He just wanted them to find this poor woman's body. And figure out what else was down in that swamp.

Near his house.

Someone had been dumping bodies near his house. Near the safest place he knew.

He shuddered.

"Would you like a c-c-copy of th-th-the photo files?" he asked Ortiz.

"Yeah," she said. "We have some computer whizzes who might find some answers here. And give me the URL for that German website, so they know this is legit."

He nodded, made copies onto a CD, and wrote down the web address for her.

She tapped him on the arm as a thank you. "This is kinda cool," she said, holding up the CD in the jewel case he'd given her. "Who knew that cats did such interesting things?"

"Yeah," DeCarovich said as he led her out the door. "Like staring at dead bodies. Who knew?"

***

HOMER COULDN'T LET DeCarovich's sarcasm and attitude get to him, even though it brought back not only Homer's high school days, but his teaching days as well. More than once, he'd caught his students in the hall, making fun of his stutter. Often they were the students from his 101 Physics class, and it was right after the unit on particles.

He had no trouble discussing electrons and protons or baryons and mesons. But quarks. Quarks caught him every time. That "ka" sound tripped him up and it got worse the longer he taught. The closer he got to the discussion of elementary particles, the more difficulty he would have.

Just like that little girl. He wished he could interview her. His stutter would put her at ease. She would be able to tell him what she saw or didn't see. She would be able to tell him how she survived when her mother hadn't.

He sighed and turned to the project at hand. He was glad he still had that sixth camera, the one the old tom had fought off. Homer was able to experiment with it. He couldn't set the timer for five seconds—it simply didn't work—but it could go off every ten seconds.

The problem was that it used a lot of energy when it took that many pictures. He found some larger memory cards, but he didn't have adequate batteries, and it was too late to buy any new ones.

So he would have to pick his times, hoping he got the right part of the day.

Then he checked his cupboards. He had a lot of canned salmon and tuna. He would need it. He would have to catch each of his feral photographers, remove their cameras, modify them, and reattach them. Then he'd have to catch the group again tomorrow and remove the memory card.

Twenty-four hours really wasn't enough.

But it was all he had.

***

By dawn, he had replaced the cameras on all of the cats.

Mata Hari was the first to return. She brought him a lovely series of photographs of the undercarriage of every car on the street. Just as the memory of the camera filled, she had crawled under a fence near the school.

He wondered if that was where she would go to get to the swamp, but he had no way of knowing.

He removed the camera, reset its automatic timer to beginning shooting later the following day, but knew it would do no good.

DeCarovich would hold to the twenty-four hour rule. The man probably still suspected Homer. Homer knew that by now, his fingerprints would have been removed from the jewel case to see if he had a criminal record (he did not) and the computer crimes unit would make sure that he hadn't dummied up the German website. They would find that he hadn't faked the website and that his cats had been taking pictures now for more than a month.

DeCarovich would also check Homer's work history, his phone usage (which was almost nil) and his bank records, which would probably surprise the detective. Popular science books made money—even if men like DeCarovich weren't interested.

Although Homer didn't know how someone like DeCarovich couldn't be interested. His job was all about science. Just on this case alone, they'd be using topographic maps and sunlight angles; they'd be removing fingerprints and studying computer records; they'd probably be using DNA to identify what was left of the other bodies.

Just by that quick reckoning, Homer figured their work would touch on geography, physics, computer science, biology, and chemistry. And all of it—even the deductive reasoning that DeCarovich was probably using to continue to blame Homer—required a meticulousness that only the best scientists could achieve.

So Homer had to hope that the other cats would bring him something, something recognizable.

Something good.

***

THE ANSWERS he sought came, surprisingly, from Einstein—a small shy male with a shock of white hair over his tiny furrowed brow. Einstein had been difficult to conquer: it had taken weeks to catch him to neuter him, and weeks after that to regain his trust. That he wore a camera at all was amazing; that he actually showed Homer the trail to the body was a shock.

Homer thought Einstein was one of the few cats who didn't make a daily pilgrimage to the swamp. Apparently he did go, just didn't stay as long as the others, and so sometimes he didn't get a good photograph. Also, Einstein was the cat whose photos were most likely to blur because he ran almost everywhere.

But on this morning, he meandered toward the swamp—through the hole in the fence that Mata Hari had found, around a stone with the year 1908 carved into the top, and then down an embankment into a copse of trees.

Einstein actually followed a tiny trail. Homer hadn't noticed it on the previous shots because it looked like a bare line in the earth, nothing spectacular. But on the ten-second shots, it was clear that the bare line was connected to other bare lines—a rabbit path that wound from the 1908 rock and into the trees.

There he saw a moss-covered old-growth stump, some ancient logging, and several late-blooming irises in front of a ruined log that Einstein crawled on top of to peer into the swamp.

The body looked worse today; less like the woman Homer had met and more like a corpse. Einstein had gotten several good pictures of it, and Homer didn't study any of them.

Instead, he copied the entire memory card onto a CD, printed the files, and called Ortiz.

She wasn't at the station. The dispatch patched him into her cell. She answered on the fourth ring, sounding annoyed.

Homer identified himself, then said, "I think I know where the path is."

"Thank God," she said. "We'll be right there."

And they were. Within fifteen minutes, they had parked in front of his house. DeCarovich looked less dyspeptic today, but Ortiz seemed frustrated.

They had been talking to the little Kemmel girl when Homer called, although "talking," DeCarovich said, "isn't really the word for it."

Homer didn't ask about it. He figured they'd tell him if they wanted to. It wasn't his investigation after all. He was just helping with one small part.

He put the printed photographs in a line, with little gaps between them. Next to them, he put a map of this section of the neighborhood.

"See this?" he said, pointing to the fence. "That's part of this house."

He pointed to a house not far from the school.

"And this rock?" he said. "It's behind the school. They christened it last year as part of a rededication. It's been there since the school was built."

He had highlighted what he believed to be the path leading into the trees.

"I figure you can use the landmarks—the irises, the old-growth stump, the log—to find her."

"You didn't look?" DeCarovich asked.

Homer frowned at him. No one in his right mind would investigate this one on his own, not when he understood the science of trace and the importance of keeping a crime scene uncontaminated.

"No," Homer said. "I figure th-th-that's your job."

The stutter surprised him. He thought he was confident enough in his map not to tighten up. But that hint of a threat in DeCarovich's voice had been enough to bring back the stutter.

"We need to go down there," DeCarovich said.

"Let's send a team," Ortiz said studying the photos.

"Let's not waste taxpayer dollars until we know we're in the right place."

For once, Homer agreed with DeCarovich. They didn't say much more to him. They took the printed photographs, the map, and the CD, and then they left.

He felt at loose ends. Despite his sensible thoughts about the crime scene, he did want to investigate it himself. He wished he were more involved.

After all, his cats had been the one to discover what Ortiz had called the body dump. If only they were trained cats. He could send them down the path to the swamp with cameras around their neck and watch as the detectives officially found Ann Kemmel's body.

But he couldn't assign the cats anything, and he could only view what they wanted to look at. Mostly, all they cared about was the undercarriage of cars.

Then he frowned and headed toward his computer. The cats loved the undercarriage of SUVs more than actual cars. SUVs had big tires and a wider frame, but a lower undercarriage than a truck. That gave the cat a lot of places to hide and even more places to visit with little feline friends, all in the comfort of a shady spot on the street.

But one photo had come to mind. A photo taken by yet another cat—Galileo—somewhere around the time of the candy selling incident. It had been a blur photo, and Homer had tossed it, but he hadn't yet cleared off the memory card.

He grabbed all the cards that needed clearing and started cycling through them one by one. He didn't find any more images of the path to the swamp—he knew he wouldn't—but he did find several of a parked SUV with unfamiliar tires.

And then he found the photograph he was looking for. Two photographs, actually. One of a skinny leg with a single pink girl's tennis shoe about to touch the pavement—and another of a pink-and-blue blur disappearing behind a bench across the street.

He closed his eyes, trying to remember what that crying girl had been wearing that afternoon. He just remembered her face, splotchy and humiliated, her eyes swollen from all the tears she'd shed. He could also remember the SUV, with its blue and silver metallic sides.

Silver, like the side where the pants leg brushed.

He opened his eyes and studied the next two frames. He didn't see any more pink and blue blurs, but he did know where that bench was. It was several doors down from his, right across the street from his surly neighbor, the man who had rolled his eyes when he'd heard the ferocity of Homer's stutter.

Homer went cold.

He wondered if he should call Ortiz. He didn't want to bother her, not when she was looking at the crime scene.

Instead, he opened a file on his computer, looked at the neighborhood map he'd downloaded earlier and studied the wetlands.

They not only ran behind his house, they ran the entire length of this side of the street, ending (or beginning depending on your point of view) at the century-old schoolhouse.

Anyone who wanted to could carry a body from their own personal back forty into the wetlands and walk through the overgrown wooded area to the swamp without being seen.

No wonder DeCarovich had suspected Homer. Homer fit all kinds of profiles. He was reclusive. He lived alone. He had access to the so-called body dump. He even inserted himself in the investigation.

His hands were shaking again. He wasn't sure if he had important information or not. The two detectives were still having trouble talking to the daughter. But Homer had evidence she left the SUV on her own and ran away.

Before or after her mother had disappeared?

He logged onto the internet and looked up what he could find on the disappearance of Ann Kemmel. She only ranked a few paragraphs in the paper on the day after her disappearance. But those few paragraphs were enough.

She and the SUV were missing.

She was last seen here on his quiet block in the middle of the afternoon on the day she disappeared, selling band candy for her daughter.

Just like he'd said.

He sank deeper into his chair. His mouth was dry. He was innocent. Ortiz knew that or she would have confiscated his computer. They would have come into his house with a warrant.

Or maybe they were waiting to find the body.

Maybe they needed just a little more for probable cause.

***

A KNOCK on the door snapped him out of his reverie. His heart was pounding and his face was already flushed. He knew he looked guilty. For all his caution, he had done so much wrong.

It would only be a matter of time before someone would come to arrest him.

He managed to leave his study, walk across his living room and peer through the glass in the door.

Ortiz stood there, arms folded behind her back. There was no sign of DeCarovich.

When she saw Homer, she nodded. She didn't smile.

Here it was: fair warning. She had come to ask if she could search his house. He would tell her to get a warrant. He would use his small fortune to hire the best criminal defense attorney in the state. He might even get his publisher's publicist to get him some interviews on his good Samaritan deed gone wrong.

He pulled open the door.

"We found her." Ortiz sounded tired. "And the others, most likely. I just wanted you to know. Your cats were right."

He waited for her to say the next part, the part about searching his house or getting a warrant. But she didn't.

She seemed to be done.

"Wow," he said. "The photos worked?"

"There was a cat path," she said. "The lab techs are down there now. It's a mess. But no one would have smelled it. Too far from houses. Too far from that school."

"The cats had to know."

"The cats must have smelled something decaying, but it didn't interest them. None of them are starving."

He smiled in spite of himself. Her comment had echoed his thoughts.

And besides, she'd seen his outdoor cats. They clearly weren't starving.

"Um," he said. "I was wondering one other thing. Th-th-that girl? Did she run away from her mother?"

Ortiz frowned at him. "How did you know?"

"I th-th-think I found some more pictures."

She came inside without asking, but she did take off her shoes. They had a swampy smell—or maybe she did—the beginnings of decay.

Princess and his other indoor cat, King, came out of the bedroom, sniffing the air. So that smell did attract them.

"I think I found pictures of the SUV," he said, and told her about the underbellies of cars, how cats socialized there, and how much they seemed to like a shady spot on the road.

"We were talking to her when you called," Ortiz said. "Poor kid. She's going to need therapy for the rest of her life."

He looked at the detective. She was already peering at the photographs on his computer.

"Why?"

"She says her mother went inside a house to sell band candy, and she ran away. She went to her grandmother's, but her grandmother brought her home."

"And no one saw the mother again."

"That's right," Ortiz said. "Missing Persons wasn't even that interested since the SUV was gone too. They figured the mother had run off."

He pointed out the skinny leg, the pink shoes, the blur of blue-and-pink across the street.

"And you know where this is, don't you?" Ortiz said.

He nodded.

She grinned at him. "Too bad we can't put those cats of yours on payroll."

"You wouldn't like them as employees," he said. "They go their own way."

And it wasn't until after she left, with more printed photographs and more files on CD, that he realized he had had an entire conversation with a woman he liked and hadn't stammered.

At least, not much.

He thought of it as a victory.

He didn't realize it was also the beginning of an odyssey.

***

ORTIZ AND DECAROVICH got a search warrant for the surly neighbor's house and found blood in the basement, and all sorts of other grisly things. The man had done exactly what Homer had hypothesized: killed the women (after abusing them sexually), then waited until dark and carried their bodies through the wetlands to the wider swampy area, dumping them there. Sometimes he would move their cars before he killed them, sometimes afterwards.

DeCarovich believed that there was a car dump like there was a body dump, but so far, no one had found it.

Ortiz kept Homer apprised of all of it. She even visited him a few times, always asking about his cats. Finally she told him she wanted to go to dinner with him, but she couldn't, not until the trial was over.

The trial. He hadn't thought of it. The grand jury, the testimony. The cross-examination.

He could already see what was coming:

He was a central part of the case—actually, his cats were—and he would feel like a failing professor all over again. Stammering his way through his stories, wishing that he could find a way to mitigate the talking part, and still explain—meticulously—his role in the arrest.

He decided to write out his testimony, to plan it, detail by detail. And as he did, he threaded the photographs through the text.

It only took him a week to figure out what he had.

A true crime book.

An unusual true crime book.

No one else had ever written anything like it.

He summoned up his courage and showed it to his agent. She loved it. She proposed a few other books as well—one just a book of photography by his cats. She showed him some curious coffee-table book from several years before of cats painting (actually just sweeping their paint-covered paws over walls and floors) and told him it had been a bestseller.

He agreed to do it all, but prosecutors wanted him to wait until his testimony was finished so that he wouldn't be accused of helping the police for money.

He wondered how anyone would think he had rigged his cameras to his feral cats for money, but he knew that people could believe anything.

So he waited. And he testified. And he did feel humiliated.

Until Detective Ortiz—her first name was Susan—took him out for a celebratory steak dinner. She had praised him, called him brilliant, and even said he was interesting.

He didn't feel interesting.

But he liked her attention.

He liked her.

He was so glad that the case had wrapped up quickly. He had been a star witness—not *the* star witness, though. That proved to be the little girl, with her father at her side, pointing out the man she'd last seen with her mother.

The surly neighbor, who no longer rolled his eyes at people who stuttered.

They had convicted him, two of the people he held in contempt. They had ended his life on the outside.

Two stammerers—two momentary stars—and five wandering cats, reluctantly sharing their secret lives bit by tiny bit.

Scrawny Pete

HE FOUND SCRAWNY PETE, flea-bitten, hair coming out in patches, and eyes like a baby's, in a fifth floor walk-up, crouched beside two dead bodies. The cat wouldn't come to anyone but him, and in a moment of weakness, he took the damn thing. The vet'd cleaned him up, put antibiotics on the scabs, gave Atkins some salve and some special food and sent him on his way.

A cat owner.

And not just any cat. Scrawny Pete was on his way to becoming a legend.

The dead bodies had been part of a domestic. Typical, in its way. Murder-suicide. Always seemed that the man shot the woman and ate the gun. Fifteen years on the crime beat for whichever daily tabloid paid him enough to write his five hundred words of wisdom showed him that there was nothing in the human existence that someone didn't try to solve with a gun. In the mouth, out of the mouth, in the heart, in the stomach, it didn't matter. In America, someone whipped out a gun and entire lives ended. A flash, an instant, leaving more heartbreak than any newspaper could cover.

As if it wanted to. Whoever said, "All happy families are alike, but all unhappy families are unhappy in their own ways," had been more right than Atkins wanted to imagine.

The problem with Scrawny Pete, as Atkins soon learned, was that the damn cat was terrified of being alone. Surprisingly, loud noises didn't bother him, and neither did the smell of blood, but his own company in the quiet of Atkins's apartment drove the cat absolutely crazy. Atkins tried leaving the television on, and bringing home a kitten, but Scrawny Pete was intelligent enough to know that a TV wasn't company, and he didn't tolerate any furry companions in his fancy abode.

Somehow the damn cat talked Atkins into taking him everywhere. Atkins started wearing a great coat with a large pocket that Scrawny Pete — who was smaller than most six-month-old kittens — took to riding in. Atkins found that Pete could be smuggled anywhere, restaurants, hotels, even doctor's offices. And once he started writing about Pete in his column, well, he didn't have to smuggle the cat anywhere any more.

It was June 21st, one year to the day after he'd gotten Scrawny Pete, that he found himself taking an old Otis to the top floor of a scrungy apartment building on the lower East Side. The cops were already on the scene. Some rookie was standing outside the main door, arms crossed, unwilling to let in any comers even with press badges until he saw Scrawny Pete. Atkins mumbled as the Otis's doors slid open on the fourteenth floor that if he'd known a cat was worth more than a press badge he'd've gotten the cat years ago.

Scrawny Pete had no answer. If anything, the cat seemed tenser than usual.

Pete was always unnaturally tense. Atkins attributed it to the poor critter's upbringing by such obviously happy folk. He could only imagine how awful it had been. The walk-up hadn't had any cat food. The only sign that a cat had even lived there were the claw marks on the living room sofa. Obviously the happy couple had let Scrawny Pete fend for his dinner in the hall with the other stray cats, and had let him the bulk of his life outside — which had probably been good for Scrawny Pete or he might have been the first to taste the gun, long before hubby decided the family needed a vacation in Never-Never-Land.

But in this hallway, which smelled of grease and garlic and Asian cooking, overlaid with filth and a bit of despair, Pete's naturally tense body became a hard little wire. Atkins put a hand on Pete's back, like he used to do when they first started traveling together, before he realized that nothing — not honking horns, not screaming people, not the breeze from a passing train — could spook Pete enough to make him leave the pocket. Pete's security was Atkins, and that cat wasn't ever going to let go.

Apartment 14A had a crooked metal sign and an open presswood door, the outside of which had once seen the backside of someone's foot. The breaks in the wood weren't new and they weren't clean, and all they left was a thin layer of really cheap oak covering between the inhabitants — or former inhabitants as the case might be — and the rest of the world.

Atkins pushed his way inside, felt Pete turn into a statue against his side and start making little huffing noises. Two detectives stood inside, both in plainclothes, cheap off-the-rack suits that had seen better days. The ME stood over the bodies with the department's camera, preserving the scene for posterity, although it was obvious what had happened.

Husband shot the wife before eating the gun. The air still had an acrid whiff from the double discharge. Atkins was surprised he could smell it over the stench of blood and voided bowels.

The detectives recognized him, showed him where to stand so that he wouldn't violate the scene. Pete was still huffing, his fur rising on his back. Strange behavior. Stranger way still to spend their one-year anniversary.

Atkins stared at the couple. Young, by the looks of their hands. Poor, by the looks of the apartment. But not that poor, by the looks of their stuff. In fact, a bit upscale for a neighborhood like this.

"Slumming, Atkins?" one of the detectives asked.

"Heard the call," he said, hand still on Pete. "What is it about this day, hm? It's not Christmas. Not nothing at all. What makes people go off on this day?"

"What?" the detective said. "There been other calls today?"

Atkins shook his head. "A year ago today, I got Pete at a place just like this one. In fact…" His voice trailed off. He shuddered, something he hadn't done at a crime scene in more than a decade.

"What?" the detective asked, but Atkins ignored him. Instead he crouched, put his hands up to his face as if he were forming a camera, and looked through the frame.

"Do bodies always fall like that in a murder-suicide?" he asked.

"Like what?" the detective asked.

"Side by side, twinned up like they're in bed next to each other, only they're on the floor."

"Naw." The answer came from the ME. He'd taken the last shot. "Usually, they are in bed. It's only a few who do it in the middle of the living room. I think they had some kind of argument, he grabs the gun, waves it in her face, she thinks he ain't gonna do nothing, maybe even dares him, he shoots, realizes what he's done, then shoots himself."

Sounded plausible.

Pete was making little sounds of distress. Atkins put his hand back in his pocket. Pete was shivering. In the whole past year, in all the strange situations, he'd never once felt Pete shiver. Not even in the middle of winter.

"Never figured you for one of them animal-lovers who took his friggin pet everywhere," the other detective said.

Atkins shrugged, pretended an indifference he didn't really feel. "It gets readers."

"Sure does," the first detective said. "The wife reads your column now like you're writing the adventures of Scrawny Pete. You should mention him every day."

"Yeah," Atkins said. "He sure has a place in a story like this one."

"I don't see no story here," the ME said. "Sad to tell, but who really cares when some guy takes out himself and his wife. 'Cept the friends and family, of course."

Atkins looked at him. The ME was a skinny redhead with premature aging lines from frowning instead of too much sunlight. "No kids?" he asked.

"Not a one."

"How common is that?"

The ME shrugged. "I'm not a walking book of statistics."

"I mean, isn't it usually long-marrieds, or newly sep-arateds, or bad divorces who resort to this?"

"Can't say." The ME looked over his shoulder. But one of the detectives frowned.

"Where you going with this, Atkins?"

"Nowhere," he said. "Just seems strange to me. The couple that I got Pete from, they were in this position, no kids, dead in the living room in a fifth floor walk-up not a lotta different from this."

"The world's weird, Atkins," one of the detectives said. "Who'd've figured? It's like you and that crazy cat."

"Yeah," Atkins said softly, not taking his hand off Pete. "Who'd've figured."

***

It DIDN'T STOP HIM from checking anyway. Superstition was sometimes a reporter's best friend. He and Pete spent the afternoon digging through records, and what he found chilled him. The past five years, there'd been a murder-suicide on the same date. Same day, same pose, different precincts. No one recognized the scene. And because it was looked like a murder/suicide, no one did more than a cursory investigation. Did he shoot her? Yeah. Did he shoot himself? Yeah. End of story.

But not really.

Atkins called the detective in charge of the latest one, told him what he'd learned, and didn't explain how he got his hunch, except to say that he remembered the anniversary of getting Pete.

Pete was still freaked. Atkins had learned, in the year he'd had Pete, that cats had memories, emotional memories, like people. The apartment drove him crazy; whenever one of the neighbors got to shouting, Pete dove under the couch. He sat in the corner like a terrified rabbit when Atkins wasn't home, not moving at all, defecating and urinating in the spot where Atkins left him in the morning. He'd done that for a week before Atkins, who knew that Pete understood a litter box, tried taking Pete to work.

The rest, of course, was history.

The detective didn't call back for two days. By then, Atkins was three columns away from the scene. He remembered it, of course. That night, Pete had slept like a baby in his arms, something he wouldn't admit to anyone, barely admitted to himself, and the cat seemed spookier than usual. But life marched on and Atkins with it, turning in his five hundred words, crime beat, the most popular column in the city with or without mention of Scrawny Pete.

"Atkins," the detective said.

"Yeah?"

"You got a story here. Want it? We wouldn'ta got it without you."

Reporters lived for calls like that. Atkins was no different, even after fifteen years. He went to the precinct, which was gray and dirty and smelled like ancient coffee, just like every other precinct in the city, and listened as the detective explained, in excruciating detail, how they went over the crime scene, how they found things that didn't exactly fit: a shoe mark in blood that didn't belong to any of the cops; a handprint on the coffee table; fibers in the wounds that had nothing to do with either deceased.

The detective didn't apologize. He knew that Atkins was a pro, Atkins understood how overworked they all were, how they liked to close cases, especially easy ones, like a murder/suicide, how hard sometimes serial killings were to see.

Luckily, or so the detective said, this one was easily solved. A neighbor — one Tobias Craig — heard the fighting, complained, complained again, finally decided to take matters into his own hands. Apparently he snapped every June 21st. Left a visible trail once they knew what to look for. Every apartment super with the June 21 murders remembered the guy complaining about the noise.

The cops had interviewed him at every scene and he'd always been the one who said the expected litany: *It don't surprise me, officers. They were fighting all the time.*

Atkins knew better than to ask for a why, but he got it anyway: Apparently Craig's name was all over the system, not as a criminal, but as a victim. Parents dead of a murder/suicide — a confirmed one — that happened in front of the children on June 21st, 1979. He'd been six at the time.

Atkins found the clippings, saw the blood-spattered children being led out of the apartment. In his imagination watched them watching their father pull out the gun like the ME had said, pull the trigger, kill his wife, then in sudden remorse, kill himself. He'd forgotten the children, sleeping in the next room, the children who'd crawled out of their shared bed to see what the noise was just in time to watch him eat his gun.

Scrawny Pete'd seen it of course. That explained the terrors, the fears of being left alone with neighbors who shouted and screamed. Was he their cat, the dead couple's? Or had he originally been a stray who'd taken food from Craig? No telling, and certainly Pete wouldn't say. Not in any way Atkins wanted to see anyway.

So he wrote the column, asked if it could go on more than 500 measly words, and because he rarely asked, and because his longer columns usually got national attention, sometimes awards, his editor said sure. Atkins wrote the story, mentioning Pete's reaction to the smells, the repeated scene. Mentioning, only mentioning. And then he'd gone on to reflect on the way the system failed the victims and the way it created more victims and was it guns or the human race's innate violence that caused a man to shoot his wife and then himself, to start a ball rolling that would leave five couples dead after some kind of terror at the hands of a crazy man who'd once been a blood-spattered six-year-old kid.

People didn't remember the analysis or the arguments or the excellent prose, some of the best of his career. Nope. They remembered the bizarre nature of the story, and they remembered Pete. And over the years, it became the crime that Pete solved, and Scrawny Pete became a legend.

Atkins didn't mind. Cats could become legends. Reporters shouldn't. Reporters schlepped from scene to scene, observing, recording, trying to make sense out of one corner of the world. Sometimes he managed it, sometimes he didn't. But he was the best at it, for a few years at least.

The years he had Scrawny Pete in his pocket.

What Fluffy Knew

*F*LUFFY KNEW she was a princess. Her person told her so. And Fluffy herself could see it, in her white, white fur, her long elegant whiskers, and her dainty paws. Fluffy had a soft bed that smelled of cedar. She had as much food as she wanted. People came to her house, and when she presented herself, they all spoke in awe of her beauty and petted her gingerly, as if they couldn't believe they were allowed to touch her sacred body. She bumped them gently to let them know that petting was preferred in her kingdom, and they usually responded with a laugh and a good ear rub.

Life was good. It didn't even matter that her people occasionally took in other cats. There had been other cats in her life as long as she was alive. She knew, however, that they weren't as great as she was. No other cat was as beautiful or as soft or as well loved. Other cats lived with her, and she tolerated them. She would have put up a large fuss, but her people had found a new palace, one with many rooms, and she rarely saw the other cats, except at feeding times.

Her routine was perfect in its simplicity. She spent her mornings in the kitchen waiting for someone to brush her, her afternoons sprawled on the couch in the warm sunshine, and her evenings on the nearest lap. Sometimes she watched the water droplets in the bathtub after her people took showers.

Nights were her special time. She prowled and explored, took food her people sometimes left near the sink, and occasionally slept on their soft bed. She was in her cedar bed at dawn just to make sure no one else used it, and then she was up, beginning her routine all over again.

Yes. It was a very good life.

Until *they* came.

***

"Please give the boys a thorough examination. I'll pay you extra. I know your time is limited when you do your house calls, and I appreciate the fact that so few vets do such a thing, but this has me bothered."

"Mrs. Winters, what's happened is tragic, but not uncommon. These adorable creatures are miniature lions. We think they're civilized, but they're not. And occasionally they remind us, often in particularly unpleasant ways."

***

They seemed to know who the weak ones were. Later, Fluffy found herself wondering: if she had known what *they* were going to do, would she have crushed *them* on that first day? Would she had stopped *them*? *They* were, after all, little bigger than a flea. But even fleas were hard to kill, weren't they? She had had fleas as a kitten, before she was elevated to her proper position, and she remembered the sudden sharp pain of the bite, the uncontrollable urge to scratch, the impossibility of catching a flea between your teeth. So perhaps she wouldn't have been able to do anything even if she had been paying attention. Even if she tried to stop the problem on the day it had started.

They went for her littermate, Streaker, and his little friend, Rook. Streaker's royal blood was diluted by his street tough father, a swaggering Tom that Fluffy barely remembered from her kittenhood. Her own father was a sweet white cat, a little on the fat side, just as her mother was. A "Pedigreed Pair," her former people used to say. The litter, they said to the people who would become her people, was ruined by the black-and-white kitten. A Tom had gotten to their precious girl at the right time. So they had to give the kittens away, unable to prove the purity of their bloodline.

Her people didn't care. They liked the black-and-white kitten with the impish streak, and they named him Streaker because he liked to run from one end of the house to the other for no apparent reason. He refused to show her the proper respect, slapping at her when she got in her way, or demanding that she give up her food. His little friend Rook, a long-haired tabby, showed many of the same behaviors. Rook was a stray her people had rescued, and to them he was kind. To her, he was as insensitive as her brother.

But she could avoid them — and often did. Streak and Rook spent most of their time together, sleeping, eating, playing. She spent most of her time with her human companions, as it should be.

So the afternoon *they* appeared, she thought nothing of it.

***

"Yes, but they've never done anything like this before. I'm beginning to wonder if something's wrong —"

"Trust me, Mrs. Winters. We get complaints like this all the time when housecats show their animal natures. There's nothing wrong."

***

It was summer. Her favorite window was open, the one overlooking the garden and the birds. She could smell flowers, which sometimes made her sneeze; other cats, which always made her curious; and birds, which usually made her want to be slightly energetic, in a wholly disgusting way. She, as her people always told her, was a princess, and didn't have to kill her own food. The boys, as her people called Streaker and Rook, didn't quite understand that, but the other two cats, Starlight and Cupcake, did. They preferred to sleep and eat, just as she did, and fortunately for her, weren't as good at attracting pets.

She had been asleep in the sun below her favorite window when *they* arrived. Rook and Streaker were sprawled in the door, playing their nasty little game: Trap Fluffy. If she hissed at them, they would jump on her and pull at her fur. If she pretended not to notice, they would leave her alone and eventually grow tired of the game. She had decided not to notice, and the hot sun had put her to sleep.

A slight whirring sound woke her up. She sat up, stretched and saw a tiny machine, rather like the ones her people watched on the box in the living room, a round machine that had doors and windows too tiny for any cat to use.

The fur rose on the back of her neck and she felt a hiss start in the back of her throat. But something warned her not to hiss. She didn't want to call attention to herself. Instead, she slipped beneath the couch, and watched.

The little door opened, and tiny human shaped creatures emerged. They were no bigger than ants. They spoke a strange language, stranger than the one her people used. It was much harder to understand. The creatures had other creatures held by silver threads — leashes as thin as spider webs and nearly as invisible. Fluffy watched as the bigger creatures unhooked the leashes, snapped their fingers, and pointed toward the door.

The smaller creatures flew across the room, like tiny flies on a mission. The larger creatures went back through the door. Fluffy heard a whirring sound, and the tiny machine was gone.

She adjusted her position under the couch, and saw the small creatures fly into Rook's left ear. Another group of them flew into Streaker's right ear.

And then the terror began.

***

"WHAT ABOUT *the alien virus?*"

"*Mrs. Winters —*"

"*Don't use that tone with me, Doctor. I've been doing some reading —*"

"*Tabloids.*"

"*They mentioned it on CNN. They said that ever since those tiny spaceships landed —*"

"*There's no proof that those are spaceships, Mrs. Winters.*"

" *— animals have been acting strangely. You told me yourself last month, when you gave Cupcake her shots that all sorts of strange things were happening to the animals in town.*"

"*I was talking about illnesses.*"

"*Well, so am I. Rook and Streaker haven't been acting normally, and I'm really worried about the other cats…*"

***

ROOK LET OUT a yelp like a cat in severe pain, and Streaker shook his head as if something were biting him.

Then they ran in opposite directions, and Fluffy didn't see them for the rest of the day.

Of course, she had to go back to sleep. The spot under the couch, despite the dirt, was much more comfortable than she had expected.

She didn't see the attack on the dog.

It was, or so her people said later in very excited tones, extremely strange. Their neighbor had brought his dog over when he came to get a package one of her admirers — the one who drove the loud brown truck — had left. Rook and Streaker bit the dog's legs and made him bleed before her people could pull them off. Her people apologized, but the neighbor got upset. Fluffy never did understand that part. It was just a dog, after all. She was more concerned about the smelly blood all over the kitchen floor.

Rook and Streaker licked it up, and smacked their lips as if they'd had a particularly tasty treat. Her male person had said it was fortunate the boys were up to date on their shots or the entire experience would have been a costly one.

The other cats chalked it up to Dog Phobia, but Fluffy didn't. She saw the look in their eyes. She had been their target many times, and she had never seen them look so sad after an attack. Usually they were gleeful. Instead, they smacked their lips and scratched their ears, and when they finally fell asleep, they whined.

A lot.

She made sure they were nowhere near her as she prowled and snacked later that night.

***

"ONE ARTICLE, *in the local paper, said a university research-er thought that the aliens were experimenting on mammals as test cases before they started experimenting on humans.*"

"*Mrs. Winters, really.*"

"*I know it sounds silly, but after what the boys did, I'm looking for any explanation. Please, Doctor. Take just a few moments. Examine them.*"

***

FOR THE FIRST THREE DAYS, they tried to get outside, but her people were too fast for them. The boys were getting older and were well fed and didn't move as fast as they used to. Their people stopped them at the door, every time, usually with a foot blocking their way. And then they turned their attention on the other cats.

Cupcake, the obese Persian who wanted Fluffy's spot as princess of the house, found a hiding spot behind the dryer. Fluffy stayed close to her people because she knew the boys wouldn't attack her in public. But Starlight, the black and gold stray, wasn't so lucky.

The boys cornered Starlight behind the toilet, and had ripped out her throat before their people could stop it. Their male person took the boys and threw them in cat carriers. Their female person tried to save Starlight. She bundled her in a towel and took her to the Emergency Vet, a place Fluffy had — fortunately — never seen.

The boys spent the night in cages in the garage. Their people promised a Mobile Vet visit in the morning. Cupcake slept well for the first time in a week.

Fluffy woke once and shivered. The boys were wailing as if they had seen the end of the world.

***

"ALL RIGHT, Mrs. Winters. I'll examine them. But before I do, let me be blunt. Starlight was a very old, malnourished stray. She wasn't part of your cat family."

"Yes, she was."

"Not to the cats. And it might not have mattered even if they had known her well. Cats live in prides and have hierarchies. And one rule that exists from lions to barn cats is that the alpha male destroys the weak so that the rest have enough to eat."

"They have enough to eat."

"It doesn't matter. It's in the genetic code."

"We've taken in strays before and they've never — you know. Killed the cat."

"Maybe the other strays weren't as sick."

"You don't think you'll find anything, do you?"

"No."

***

FLUFFY HATED PUZZLES, and she really didn't like the boys. They harassed her and didn't give her the respect that royalty deserved. But she didn't like to hear anyone cry either. And her person was right: they hadn't killed Starlight. Those creatures inside them had.

She had to get those creatures out of the boys. And she had to do it without infecting herself or Cupcake.

The creatures had gone in the ear. The Mobile Vet had cold wet stuff that went in the ear. She had seen him use it on Starlight just last week. Maybe that would be enough to get the creatures out.

But how to tell her person and the Mobile Vet what she knew? They would think, if she wound around their legs, that she wanted pets. And even though they thought themselves superior, they never had mastered Fluffy's language, not like she had mastered theirs. The problem was she couldn't speak it; she hadn't seen the use for it until now.

Her person had brought Streaker in from the garage. He had dried blood on his muzzle and his eyes were wide and dark. He looked like a cat in pain to Fluffy.

Her person put Streaker's cat carrier on the kitchen counter, and started to open the gate. Fluffy had to act now. She took a flying leap — something she hadn't done since she was a kitten — and landed on the Vet's medical bag.

He made a small sound and her person spoke her name in that sharp reprimanding tone. Fluffy ignored her. Instead she scratched on the top of the bag until a corner of it pulled back. She put a paw under it, and clung as the vet tried to lift her off.

Instead, he helped her open the bag.

There were rows of needles inside, and lots of little vials. She tried not to watch when he worked on the other cats, and she could barely remember what he had done to Starlight's ear.

He hadn't used a needle. He had used a bottle. A small white bottle that liquid dripped out of.

She only had a moment. She batted a bottle aside, and it rolled along the floor. Then she wriggled out of the vet's grasp and jumped on the counter.

Her person reprimanded her again. Fluffy stopped in front of Streaker's cage and scratched her ear. He frowned at her. She scratched her other ear, and her person shoved her on the floor.

She landed with an unceremonious thump, and she had to pause to lick herself. No princess ever allowed herself to be shoved like that, not even in the name of justice.

From above, she heard the sound of a back foot thumping against a plastic cage.

Streaker had understood.

***

"*They're too big to be earmites.*"

"*Then what are they?*"

"*I don't know. But I'm going to take them to the lab with me and investigate. I'll leave this vial with you. If you see any more of them, scoop them up and bring them to me. Don't let them near the cats.*"

"Should we do the other cats?"

"Probably. Yes. Get them. We'd best make sure this is taken care of. Something this big in your ear would be painful. We don't want it to happen again."

***

FOR HER TROUBLES, she was grabbed, held by the scruff of the neck, and had cold liquid shoved down her ear, with instructions to have the same procedure repeated until the liquid was gone. Both the vet and her person were pleased to see that no creatures came out of her ears.

And then they went off to find Cupcake.

Streaker looked at her from his cage. She looked back. His eyes closed slowly. She had never seen a cat seem so exhausted — and so relieved.

***

"DOCTOR?"

"Mmm?"

"Are those bugs what made my boys kill Starlight?"

"I can't answer that for sure, Mrs. Winters. I don't know what these bugs are or what they do."

"But the boys, will they hurt my other cats?"

"Cats aren't like dogs, Mrs. Winters. Once dogs get a taste for blood, they usually must be kept outside or destroyed. Cats — the thing that your cats did — is natural. They hurt things *one minute and cuddle with their owner the next. Will your cats be the same loving creatures you've always known? Of course. Will they hurt Cupcake and Fluffy? Not unless they get so sick that they're a threat to the pride. I would say that you separate your cats in the future when one of them gets ill. That'll ensure something like this will never happen again."*

"So I can let them have the run of the house, and they won't hurt anyone again?"

"If you follow my instructions."

"I will. Oh, Doctor. How will I ever forgive them for Starlight?"

"Realize they're not human, and that human laws don't apply. What they did was right in the feline world."

"That doesn't work for me."

"Then blame it on the bugs."

***

THREE DAYS LATER, Fluffy was asleep in the sun beneath her favorite window. The boys were cuddled on the couch, still exhausted from their ordeal.

A whir woke Fluffy up. She rolled over and saw the tiny machine on the windowsill. The little door opened and the bigger creatures came out. They held tiny whistles in their hands.

The high-pitched sound woke up the boys. They glanced at Fluffy. She glanced at them. Then she reached up with one paw, and knocked the machines — and the bigger creatures — off the sill.

The boys jumped down beside her, and the hunt began.

It was Rook who discovered that if you bit one of the creatures halfway between its head and its feet and then threw it against the wall, it didn't move again. Streaker discovered that a paw through the door crushed the little machines.

But Fluffy was the one who figured out how to knock down machines mid-flight; Fluffy who figured out how to dodge the tiny rays of light that hurt more than a needle's prick; Fluffy who figured out how to flush the machines down the toilet so that they would be gone for good.

Because Fluffy knew if the creatures and their tiny machines succeeded in taking over Rook and Streaker, they might take over her. And if they took over her, and discovered how wonderful her life was, it wouldn't be long before they sent for more little machines and sent bugs into the ears of her people. And once they had control of her people, they had control of the entire world.

And Fluffy couldn't let that happen. In this world, she was a princess. And she would remain a princess — even if it meant dirtying her paws to do so.

The creatures hadn't known what they were up against.

But Fluffy knew.

And Fluffy won.

Just like she knew she would.

The Poop Thief

"**O**KAY, THIS is just weird."

The voice came from the back of the store. It belonged to my Tuesday/Thursday assistant, Carmen. High school student, daughter of two mages, Carmen had no real talent herself, but she was earnest, and she loved creatures, and I loved her enthusiasm.

"I mean it, Miss Meadows, this is weird."

Oddly enough, weird is not a word people often use in Enchantment Place. Employees expect weird. Customers demand it. What's weird here is normal everywhere else—or so I thought until that Tuesday in late May.

"Miss Meadows…."

"Hold on, Carmen," I said. "I'm with a client."

The client was a repeat whom I did not like. I'm duty bound at Familiar Faces to provide mages with the proper familiars—the ones that will help them augment their talents and help them remain on the right path (doing no harm, avoiding evil, remaining true to the cause, all that crap). I do my best, but some people try my patience.

People like Zhakeline Jones. She was a zaftig woman who wore flowing green scarves, carried a cigarette in a cigarette holder, and called everyone "darling." Even me.

I called her Jackie, and ignored the "It's Zhakeline, dahling." Actually, it was Jacqueline back when we were in high school and then only from the teachers. The rest of us called her Jackie, and her friends—what few she had—called her Jack.

Whenever she came in, I cringed. I knew the store would smell like cigarettes and Emerude perfume for days afterwards. I didn't let her smoke in here—Enchantment Place, for all its oddities, was regulated by the City of Chicago and the City of Chicago had banned smoking in all public places—but that didn't stop the smell from radiating off her.

Most of my creatures vacated the front of the store when she arrived. Only the lioness remained at my feet, curled around my ankles as if I were a tree and Zhakeline was her prey. A few of the mice looked down on Zhakeline from a shelf (sitting next to the books on specialty cheeses that I'd ordered just for them), and a couple of the birds sat like fat and sassy gargoyles in the room's corners.

Nothing wanted to go home with Zhakeline, and I didn't blame them. She'd brought back the last three familiars because the creatures had the audacity to sneeze when they entered her house (and silly me, I had thought that cobras couldn't sneeze, but apparently they do—especially when they don't want to stay in a place where the air is purple). We were going to have to find her something appropriate and tolerant, something I was beginning to believe impossible to do.

On the wall beside me, lights shimmered from all over the spectrum, then Carmen appeared. Actually, she'd stepped through the portal from the back room to the shop's front, but I'd specifically designed the magical effect to impress the civilians.

Sometimes it impressed me.

Carmen was a slender girl who hadn't yet grown into her looks. One day, her dramatic bone structure would accent her African heritage. But right now, it made her look like someone had glued an adult's cheekbones onto a child's face.

"Miss Meadows, really, my parents say you shouldn't ignore a magical problem and I think this is a magical problem, even though I don't know for sure, but I'm pretty certain, and I'm sorry to bother you, but jeez, I think you have to look at this."

All spoken in a breathless rush, with her gaze on Zhakeline instead of on me.

Zhakeline smiled sympathetically and waved a hand in dismissal. Bangles that had been stuck to her skin loosened and clanked discordantly.

"This hasn't really been working, Portia." Zhakeline said with a tilt of the head. She probably meant that as sympathy too. "I've been thinking of going to that London store—what do they call it?"

"The Olde Familiar." I spoke with enough sarcasm to sound disapproving. Actually, my heart was pounding. I would love it if Zhakeline went elsewhere. Then the unhappy familiar—whoever the poor creature might be—wouldn't be my responsibility.

"Yes, the Olde Familiar." She smiled and put that cigarette holder between her teeth. She bit the damn thing like a feral F.D.R. "I think that would be best, don't you?"

I couldn't say yes, because I wasn't supposed to turn down mage business and I could get reported. But I didn't want to say no because I would love to lose Zhakeline's business.

So I said, "You might try that store in Johannesburg too, Unfamiliar Familiars. You can see all kinds of exotics. But remember, importing can be a problem."

"I'm sure you'll help with that," she said.

"Legally I can't. But you're always welcome here if their wares don't work out."

The mice chittered above me, probably at the word "wares." They weren't wares and they weren't animals. They were sentient beings with magic of their own, subject only to the whims of the magical gods when it came to pairings.

The whims of the magical gods and Zhakeline's eccentricities.

"I'll do that," she said. Then she turned to Carmen. "I hope you settle your weirdness, darling. And for the record, your parents *are* right. The sooner you focus on a magical problem, the less trouble it can be."

With that, she swept out of the store. Two chimpanzees crawled through the cat doors on either side of the portal holding identical cans of Fabreeze.

"No," I said. "The last time you did that we had to vacate the premises. Or don't you remember?"

They sighed in unison and vanished into the back. I didn't blame them. The smell was awful. But Fabreeze interacted with the Emerude, leading me to believe that what Zhakeline wore wasn't the stuff sold over the counter, but something she mixed on her own.

Without a familiar, which was probably why the stupid stuff lingered for days.

"Miss Meadows." Carmen tugged on my sleeve. "Please?"

I waved an arm so that the store fans turned on high. I also uttered an incantation for fresh ocean breezes. (I'd learned not to ask for wind off Lake Michigan; that nearly chilled us out of the store one afternoon). Then I followed Carmen into the back.

Walking through the portal is a bit disconcerting, especially the first time you do it. You are walking into another dimension. I explain to civilian friends that the back room is my Tardis. Those friends who don't watch *Doctor Who* look at me like I'm crazy; the rest laugh and nod.

My back room should be a windowless 10x20 storage area. Instead, it's the size of Madison Square Garden. Or two Madison Square Gardens. Or three, depending on what I need.

Most of my wanna-be familiars live here, most of them in their own personal habitats. The habitats have a maximum requirement, all mandated by the mage gods and tailored to a particular species. Each bee has a football-sized habitat; each tiger has about a half an acre. Most creatures may not be housed with others of their kind, unless they're a socially needy type like herding dogs or alpha male cats. The creatures have to learn how to live with their mage counterparts—not always an easy thing to do—and its best not to let them interact too much with other members of their species.

Theoretically, I get the creatures after they complete five years of familiar training (and yes, you're right; very few familiars live their normal lifespan. Insects get what to them seems like millions of years and dogs get an extra two decades; only elephants, parrots, and a few other exceptionally long-lived species live a normal span).

That day, I had too many monkeys of various varieties, one parrot return who'd managed to learn every foul word in every language known to man (and I mean that) during his aborted tenure with his new owner, several large predatory cats, twenty-seven butterflies, five gazelle, sixteen North American deer, eight white wolves, one black bear, one grizzly return, one-hundred domestic cats, five-hundred-sixty-five dogs, and dozens of other creatures I generally forgot when I made a mental list.

Not every animal was for sale. Some were flawed returns—meaning they couldn't remember spells or they misquoted incantations or they weren't temperamentally suited to such a high-stress job. Some were whim returns, brought back by the mage who either bought on a whim or returned on a whim. And the rest were protest returns. These creatures left their mage in protest, either of their treatment or their living conditions.

All three of Zhakeline's returns had been protest returns although she tried to pass the first off as a flaw return and the other two as whim returns. It gets hard for a mage after a few rejections. Eventually she gets a reputation as a familiarly challenged individual, and might never get a magical companion.

And if she goes without for too long, she'll have her powers suspended until she goes through some kind of rehab.

Fortunately, that's never my decision. I'd seen too many mages fight to save their powers just before a suspension: I never want all that angry magic directed at me.

Carmen was standing on the edge of the habitats. They extended as far as the eye could see. My high school assistants didn't tend the habitats the way that civilian high school assistants would tend cages at, say, a vet's office. Instead, they made sure that the attendants that I hired from various parts of the globe (at great expense) actually did their jobs.

Each attendant had to log in stats: food consumed, creature health readings, and how often each habitat was entered, inspected, and cleaned. Then they'd log in the video footage for the past day—after inspecting it, of course, for magical incursions, failed spells, or escape attempts.

Carmen had called up our stats on the clear computer screen I'd overlaid over the habitat viewing area. She zoomed in on one stat—product for resale.

I frowned at the numbers. They were broken down by category. The whim returns and most of the protest returns were listed, of course, along with byproduct—methane from the cows (to be used in various potions); shed peacock feathers (for quills); and honey from the bees that had convinced the mage gods to make them hive familiars, not individual familiars.

Those bees only went to special clients—those who could prove they weren't allergic and who could handle several personality types all speaking through their fearless leader, the sluggish queen.

"See?" Carmen asked, waving a hand at the numbers. "This week's just weird."

I didn't see. But I didn't have as much experience with the numbers as she did. And, truth be told, I didn't think her powers were in spell-casting. I believed they were in numerology—not as powerful a magic, but a useful one.

"I'm sorry," I said, feeling dense, like I often did when staring at rows of facts and figures. "What am I supposed to see?"

She poked her finger at one of the columns. The lighted numbers vanished, then reappeared in red.

"Available fertilizer," she said. "See?"

I stared at the category. Available Fertilizer. Our biggest seller because we undercut the competition, mostly so we could get rid of the crap quickly and easily.

"There's no number there," I said.

"Zero is a number," Carmen said with dripping disdain that only a teenager could muster.

"E…yeah…okay." I knew I was stammering, but the big honking nothingness made no sense. "The assistants haven't been cleaning the habitats?"

She pressed the screen, drawing down the earlier statistics. Cleanings had gone on as usual.

"So what happened to the fertilizer?"

"I have no idea where the fertilizer went," she said. "I'm not even sure it came out of the cages. I mean, habitats."

I had planned to give her a tour of the back, but I hadn't yet. So she always made the "cages/habitat" mistake, something she'd never say if she actually saw the piece of the Serengeti plain that Fiona, the lioness who liked to sleep under my cash register and Roy, the lion who supposedly headed her pride, had conjured up to remind themselves of home.

Cleaning the habitats was a major job, especially for the larger animals, and usually required extra labor. Entire families came in for an hour or two a night to clean grizzly's mountainside, especially during blackberry season.

I moved Carmen aside, pressed some keys only visible to me, and looked at several of the previous day's vids in fast motion. Habitat cleaning happened in all of them.

Habitat cleaners weren't required to log in what they cleaned unless the item was marketable which poop generally was. Animal poop that is. There's never a big market for insect poop.

Animal poop (ground up into a product called Familiar Fertilizer) had a wide variety of uses. Mages bought it for their herb gardens. In addition to being the

Miracle Grow of the magical world, it also made sure that wolf's bane and all the other herbal ingredients of a really good potion, magical spell, or "natural" remedy was extra-powerful. Some mages vowed that anything fertilized with familiar poop could be safely sold with a money-back guarantee—especially (oddly enough) love spells.

"Must be a computer glitch," I said and stabbed a few more buttons.

"Let me." Carmen got to the correct screens quicker, without me even asking. She knew I wanted to check all that basic stuff—how many pounds of poop got ground into fertilizer at the nearby processing plant, how many pounds of fertilizer got shipped, and how many of our magical feed-and-seed brethren paid for shipments that arrived this week.

Each category had a big fat zero in the poundage column.

"I don't like this," I said. "You just noticed this?"

I tried to keep the accusation out of my voice. It wasn't her job to keep track of my shipments and my various product lines. She was a high school student working two days a week part-time after school.

I was the person in charge.

"I was going over the manifests like you taught," she said. "I let you know the minute I saw it."

Which was—I checked the digital readout on the see-through computer screen—half an hour ago, one hour after Carmen arrived.

Pretty dang fast, considering.

"I mean, everything was fine on Thursday."

Thursday. The last day she worked.

My lunch—an indulgent slice of Chicago pan-style pizza—turned into a gelatinous ball in my stomach. "Can you quickly check the previous four days?"

"Already on it." She pressed a few keys.

I watched numbers flash in front of my eyes—too quickly for my number-challenged brain to follow. I could have spelled the whole thing, looked for patterns, but I had Carmen. She was better than any magical incantation.

"Wow," she said after a few minutes. "Those animals haven't pooped since Friday."

The gelatinous ball became concrete. I reached for the screen to look at health history, then stopped. A few of those creatures would have died if they hadn't pooped in three days. Some internal systems were less efficiently designed than others.

Still, I had her double-check the health records just to make sure.

"Okay," she said after looking at health records from Thursday to Tuesday. "So they all have normal bowel readings. What does this mean?"

"It means that your parents are right," I said.

"Huh?" She looked at me sideways, all teenager again. She hated hearing that Mom and Dad were right.

"Magical problems become bigger when they are allowed to fester."

"This is a magical problem?" she asked.

"The worst," I said.

She continued to stare at me in confusion, so I clarified.

"We have a poop thief."

***

YOU FIND POOP THIEVES throughout magical literature. Heck, you even find them in fairy tales.

Of course, they're never called poop thieves. They're "tricksters" who steal their victims' "essence." They're evil wizards who rob their enemies of their "life force."

Most scholars believe that these references are to sperm, which simply tells me that magical scholarship has been dominated too long by males. (Those inept male scholars don't seem to be able to read either; a lot of the victims are women who are, of course, spermless creatures one and all.)

The scholars are right in that "life force" and "essence" are often composed of bodily fluids. Some (female) scholars have assumed that this essence is blood, but blood is a lot harder to obtain than the simplest of bodily fluids—pee.

Pee, though, is like all other water. It seeps into the ground. It's difficult to get unless someone pees into a cup or a bottle or a box. (Or unless you've magicked the chamberpot—and there are a few of those stories as well [Those Brothers Grimm didn't like the chamberpot stories, and so kept them out of the official compilation.])

Poop, on the other hand…

Poop, actually, on either hand is a lot easier to obtain.

Poop, like pee, blood, and yes, sperm, is a life essence. Even in its nonmagical form it has magical powers. It gets discarded only to be spread on a fallow field. The nutrients in the waste material break down, enriching the soil which is often used to grow plants—plants which later become food. The food nourishes the person who eats it. The person's body processes the food into energy and vitamins and all sorts of other good stuff, and the leftovers become waste yet again.

Most of the non-magical have no idea the power held in a single turd.

Hell, most of the magical didn't either.

But the ones who did, well, they were all damn dangerous.

And I'd already lost too much time.

***

IT SEEMED ODD to call Mall Security at a time like this, but that was the first thing I did. Mine wasn't the only store with magical creatures.

If someone was stealing from me, then maybe he was stealing from the pet store down the way, the organ grinder monkey show just outside the food court, and the various holiday setups with their real Easter bunnies and Christmas reindeer and Halloween bats. Not to mention all the working familiars accompanying every single mage who walked into the place.

I let Carmen talk to Security. She was young enough and naïve enough to think they were sexy. She had no idea that most of them were failed magical enforcers or inept warlocks who'd been demoted from city-wide security patrol to Enchantment Place.

I stayed in the back room, bending a few rules because this was an emergency. Anyone who took that much poop had a plan. A big plan—or a need for a lot of power.

At first, I figured this thief simply wanted the magical support of a familiar without actually getting a familiar. Magical crime blotters were full of minor poop thieves who stole rather than get a new familiar of their own. They'd mine someone else's familiar, using the poop as a tool with which to obtain the magic, and no one would notice until that familiar got sick from putting out too much magical energy.

Maybe what we had here was a more sophisticated version of the neighborhood poop snatcher.

Which made Zhakeline a prime suspect.

But Zhakeline's magic had always been shaky at best, even when she had a familiar. That was why she looked so exotic and had so many affectations.

She had to appeal to the civilians who think we're all weird. She mostly sold her small magic services to them. If she predicted the future and was wrong or if she made a love potion that didn't work, the civilian would simply shrug and think to himself *Ah, well, magic doesn't really work after all.*

But the magical, we know when someone can't perform all of the spells in the year-one playbook. Zhakeline barely passed year one (charity on the part of the instructor) and shouldn't have passed from that point on. But that happened during the years when telling a kid that she had failed was tantamount to murdering her (or so the parents thought) and Zhakeline got pushed from instructor to instructor without learning anything.

Which was one of the many reasons I didn't want to give her another familiar.

And that was beside the point.

The point was that Zhakeline, and mages like her—the ones who needed the magical power of familiar poop—didn't have the ability to conduct a theft on this massive scale, at least not alone.

And even if they tried, they'd be better off going to the back yard of a mage with a canine familiar. There was always a constant poop supply, and it provided enough power—consistent power (from the same source)—so that the thief might become a slightly less inept mage, for a while, anyway.

Next I investigated my assistants. Most had no magical powers of their own, but had come from magical families. They knew that magic existed—and not in that hopeful *I wish it were so* way that a civilian had, but in a *this is a business* way that led them to peripheral jobs in the magical field.

They worked hard, most had a love of animals, insects or reptiles, and they often had a specialty—whether it was cooking the right kind of pet food or calming a petulant hyena.

I couldn't believe any of the assistants would be doing something like this because they would have to be working for someone else.

The nonmagical don't gain magic just by wishing on a powerful piece of poop.

I scanned records and employment histories. I scanned bank accounts (yes, that's illegal, but remember—emergency. A few rules needed to be bent), cash stashes and (embarrassingly) the last 48 hours of their lives. (Which, viewed at the speed of an hour per every ten seconds, looked like silent movies watched at double fast-forward.)

I saw nothing suspicious. And believe me, I knew what to look for.

Although I wished I didn't.

***

YOU SEE, I got this job, not because I have a particular affinity with animals or I'm altruistic and love pairing the right mage with the right familiar.

I got it because I have experience.

I know how to look for mages heading dark or mages who should retire or mages who mistreat their magic (and hence their familiars). I know how to take care of these mages quietly, efficiently, and with a minimum of fuss.

It didn't used to be this way. In the past, places like Familiar Faces existed on side streets and had just a handful of creatures, few of them exotic. Only in the last few years have the mega stores come into existence at high-end malls like Enchantment Place.

And even though we're supervised by the rules of the mage gods like all other familiar stores, we're run and subsidized by Homeland Security—Magical Branch.

(Not everyone knows there's a Homeland Security—Magical Branch, including the so-called "head" of Homeland Security. Hell, I even doubt the president knows. Why tell the person who's going to be out in four or eight years one of the world's most important secrets. Knowing this crew, they'd probably try to co-opt the Magical Branch into something dark. Better to keep quiet and protect us all.

(Which I do. Most of the time.)

My job here is to watch for exactly this kind of incursion. Technically, I'm supposed to report it, and then wait for the guys with badges to show up.

But I didn't wait for the guys with badges. I doubted we would have time.

(And, truth be told, I did want the glory. I was demoted to this position [you guessed that already, right?] for asking too many questions and for the classic corporate mistake, proving that the boss was an idiot in front of his employees. I'm a government employee and as such can't be fired without lots and lots of red tape [even in the magical world], so I was sent here, to Chicago where I grew up, to Enchantment Place where I have to put up with the likes of Zhakeline with a smile and a shrug and a rather pointed [and sometimes magically directed] suggestion.)

I toyed with rewinding time in all of the habitats—another no-no, but it would have been protected under the Patriot Act, like most no-nos these days. But rewinding time takes time, time I didn't really want to waste looking at creatures moping in their personal space.

Instead, I did some old-fashioned police work.

I went back out front where Carmen was still flirting with some generic security guard (and the mice were leaning over so far to watch that I was afraid one of them would fall down the poor man's ill-fitting shirt) and beckoned the lioness, Fiona.

She frowned at me, then rose slowly, stretched in that boneless way common to all cats, and padded through the portal ahead of me.

When I got back to the back, she was sitting on her haunches and cleaning her ears, as if she had meant to join me all along.

"We have a poop thief," I said, "and I think you know who it is."

She methodically washed her left ear, then she started to lick her left paw in preparation for cleaning her right ear.

"Fiona," I said, "if I don't solve this, something bad will happen. You might not get a home of any kind and none of the other familiars will be of use to anyone. You might all have to be put down."

I usually don't use euphemisms, and Fiona knew it. But she didn't know the reason that I used it this time.

I couldn't face killing all these wanna-be familiars. And it would be my job to do so. I'd get blamed for the theft(s), and I'd have to put down the creatures affected. It was the only way to negate the power of their poop.

She put her newly cleaned paw down on the concrete floor. "You couldn't 'put us down.'" She used great sarcasm on the phrase. "It would set the magical world back more than a hundred years. There wouldn't be enough of us to help your precious mages perform their silly little spells."

"Which might be the point of this attack," I said. "So tell me what you saw the last few days."

And why you never said a word, I almost added, but didn't.

"I'm not supposed to tell you anything. I'm not even supposed to talk with you."

Technically true. Familiars are only supposed to talk to their personal mages. But I get to hear and every one of them speak when they come into the store to make sure they really are familiars and not just plain old unmagical creatures looking for a free hand-out.

But Fiona had spoken to me before, mostly sarcastic comments about the store patrons. I'd tried pairing her up with a few, but she always had an under-the-breath comment that convinced me she and that mage wouldn't be a good match.

"I haven't seen anything," she said.

"What have you heard, then?" I asked.

"Nothing," she said. "The system is working just fine."

That sarcasm again, which lead me to believe she was leaving out a detail or two deliberately, hoping I would catch it.

Damn lions. They're just giant cats. They toy with everything.

And at that moment, Fiona was toying with me.

"But something's bothering you," I said.

"Not me so much." She picked up that clean right paw, turned it over, and examined the claws. "Roy."

Roy was the lion to her lioness. He wasn't head of the pride because there was no pride. We knew better than to get an entire pride of lions into that small habitat. No one would ever be able to see their individual natures—and no mage was tough enough to get that many catly familiars.

"What's bothering Roy?" I asked.

"Ask him."

"Fiona…"

She nibbled on one of the claws, then set her paw down again. "There was—oh, let me see if I can find the phrase in your language—an overpowering scent of ammonia."

"Ammonia?"

"And a very bright light."

"An explosion?" I asked. Fertilizer mixed with the right chemicals, including ammonia, created the same thing in both the magical and the non-magical world.

A bomb.

Only the magical bomb made of this kind of fertilizer didn't just destroy lives and property, it also cut through dimensions.

"It's not an explosion yet," she said. "He claims he has a sixth sense about things. Or did he say he can see the future? I forget exactly. But it was something like that."

"Or maybe he just knows something," I snapped.

"Or maybe he just knows something." She sounded bored. "He does say that because he's king of the jungle, the wanna-bes tell him things."

Which was the most annoying thing about Roy. He really believed that king of the jungle crap. Too much Kipling as a cub—or maybe too many viewings of the *Lion King.*

"I should really send you back to the habitat until this is resolved," I said to Fiona.

She hacked like she had a hairball, a sound she (sort of) learned from me. She thought it was the equivalent of my very Chicago, very dismissive "ach."

"I'd rather be out front, watching the floor show," she said.

And I sent her back out there because I had a soft spot for Fiona. Technically, I don't need a familiar. I have more than a thousand of them.

But if I did need one, I'd pick Fiona.

She knew it and she played on it all the damn time.

I waited until she was through that little curtain of light before I stepped through the hidden door into the habitat area.

It was always surprisingly quiet inside the habitat area. The first time I went in, I expected chirping birds and chittering monkeys and barking dogs—a cacophony of creature voices expressing displeasure or loneliness or sheer cussedness.

Instead, the area was so quiet that I could hear myself breathe.

It also had no smell—unless you counted that dry scent of air conditioning. The animal smells—from the pungent odor of penguins to the rancid scent of coyote—existed only in the individual habitat.

Just like the noises did.

If I went through the membrane on my left (and only I could go through those membranes—or someone I had approved, like the assistants), I would find myself in a cold dark cave that smelled of rodent and musty water. If I looked up, I'd see the twenty-seven bats currently in inventory.

We were always understocked on bats. Mages, particularly young ones raised in Goth culture, wanted bats first, wolves second, and cats a distant third. I'd given up trying to tell those kids to get some imagination.

I'd given up trying to tell the kids anything.

If I went through the membrane on my right, I'd slide on polar ice. Here the ice caps weren't melting. Here, my six polar bears happily fished and scampered and did all those things polar bears do—except that they didn't attack me. They didn't even bare their fangs at me.

I stopped between the two membranes and frowned. Whoever took the poop hadn't taken it from inside the habitats. It was simply too dangerous for the unapproved guest.

Hell, it was often dangerous for the assistants. I'd had more than one assistant mauled by a creature that didn't like the way he was looking at it.

And the poop was not registered as collected either. So whoever had taken it had spelled it out between gathering and delivery into the outside system.

I walked between dozens of habitats, trying to ignore the curious faces watching me.

I did feel for the wanna-bes. They were like children in an old-fashioned orphans' home. They hoped that someone would come to adopt them. They prayed that someone would come to adopt them. They were afraid that someone had come to adopt them.

And the only way they would know was if I brought them out of the habitat to the front of the store. (Except in the case of the dangerous exotics or the biting/stinging insects. In those cases, the mage had to enter the habitat without fear. *That* rarely happened either.)

Finally I got to the Serengeti Plain.

Or what passed for it in Roy and Fiona's habitat. It was kind of an amalgam of the best parts of a lion's world minus the worst part. Lots of water, lots of space to run, lots of space to hide. A great deal of sunshine and never, ever any rain.

I slipped through the membrane and, because of my past experience, paused.

The first step into Roy's world was overwhelming. The heat (about twenty degrees higher than I ever liked, even in the summer), the smell (giant cat mixed with dry grass and rotting meat from the latest kill), and the sunlight (so bright that my best sunglasses were no match for it—and as usual, I had forgotten any sunglasses) all made for a heady first step into this habitat.

More than one assistant had been so disoriented by the first step that Roy was able to tackle, stand on, and threaten the assistant in the first few seconds. After you've had several hundred pounds of lion standing on your chest, with his face inches from yours—so close you could see the pieces of raw meat still hanging from his fangs—you'd never want to go back into that habitat either.

Unless you're me, of course. I expected Roy to scare me that first time.

I didn't expect him to catch me off guard.

So when he did, I congratulated him, told him he was quite impressive, and warned him that if he hurt a human he'd never graduate from wanna-be to familiar.

And from that point on, he never jumped on me again.

But he always snuck up on me.

On this day, he wrapped his giant mouth around my calf. His teeth scraped against my skin, his hot breath moist and redolent of cat vomit. He'd been eating grass again. We were going to have change his diet.

"Hey, Roy," I said. "I hear you have a sixth sense."

He tightened his jaw just enough that the edges of those sharp teeth would leave dents in my flesh—not quite bites, not quite bruises—for days. Then he licked the injured area—probably an apology, or maybe just a taste for salt (I was instant sweat any time I came into this place).

Finally, he circled around me and climbed a nearby rock so that he would tower over me. If I weren't so used to his power games, he'd make me nervous.

"It's not a sixth sense," he said in an upperclass British accent. That accent had startled me when we were introduced. "So much as a finely honed sense of the possible."

"I see," I said, because I wasn't sure how to respond. I hadn't even been certain he would talk to me, and he'd done so almost immediately.

Which led me to believe the king of the jungle was more terrified than he wanted to admit.

"You realize I am only speaking to you," he said with an uncanny ability to read my mind (or maybe it was just that finely honed sense of what I might possibly be thinking), "because great evil is afoot, and I have no magical counterpart with which to fight it."

I almost said, *It's not your job to fight it,* but I didn't. I didn't want to insult the poor beast. Instead, I said, "That's precisely why I'm here. I figured you know what was going on."

"Bosh," he said. "Fiona told you. She has a thing for you, you know."

"A thing?" I asked.

"She wants to be your familiar." He opened his mouth in a cat-grin. "She doesn't understand—or perhaps she doesn't believe—that you have hundreds of us and as such do not need her."

I nodded because I wasn't sure what else to do. And because I was already thirsty. I'd forgotten not just my sunglasses but my bottle of water as well.

"Well," I said, "you do know what's happening, right?"

"Oh, bomb-making, dimension hopping, familiar murder—all the various possibilities." He laid down and crossed his front paws as if none of that bothered him. "And just you here because you seem to believe that you can save the world all by your own small self."

"With the help of your finely honed sense of the possible."

"That too." He tilted his massive head and looked at me through those slanted brown eyes.

My heart rate increased. Occasionally I still did feel like prey around him.

"Well?" I asked.

"Have you ever thought that your culprit isn't human?"

"No," I said. "Demons don't care about familiars. Only mages do."

"Really." He extended the word as if it were four. "Humans generally ignore scat, don't they?"

"Generally," I said. "We try not to think about it."

"And yet those of us in the animal kingdom find within it a wealth of information."

"Yes," I said. "But the amount of power it would take to complete this spell tends to rule out anything that isn't human."

He made the same hairball sound that Fiona did. They were closer than they liked to admit.

"You humans are such speciest creatures. It doesn't help that the mage gods allow you the choices and we have to wait until you make them. It leads me to believe that the mage gods are human—or were, at one point."

I wasn't there to discuss religion. "You're telling me, then, that your finely honed sense of the possible leads you to the conclusion that a familiar has done this."

"I didn't say that."

"A creature then. A magical creature of some kind."

He slitted his eyes, the feline equivalent of yes.

"But you have no evidence," I said.

"I have plenty of evidence. Consider the timeline. It took you forever to discover this theft, and yet no bomb has exploded. No one has made threats, and no mage has suddenly gained unwarranted power."

"That's not evidence. That's supposition."

He lifted his majestic head. "Is it?"

"So who do you suppose has stolen the poop—and why?"

He rested his head on his paws and continued to stare at me. "That's for you to work out."

"In other words, you don't know."

"That's correct. I don't really know."

"But you're not worried."

"Why should I worry? From my perspective, removing the scat is a prudent thing to do."

I hadn't expected him to say that. "What do you mean?"

He heaved a heavy, smelly sigh. "I'm a cat who lives in the wild. Think it through."

Then he jumped and I cringed as he headed right toward me. He landed beside me, chuckled and vanished through the tall grass.

He'd gotten me again. He loved that. He'd probably been planning to jump near me through the entire conversation, his back feet tucked beneath him and poised, even though his front half looked relaxed.

He wasn't going to give me any more. He felt he didn't need to.

Cats in the wild.

Cat poop in the wild.

Hell, cat poop in the house. Cats were all the same.

They buried their poop so no one could track them.

The problem wasn't the poop thief.

The poop thief was protecting the wanna-bes from something else. Something that tracked through scat.

Something that wasn't human.

I swore and bolted out of the habitat.

I needed my research computer, and I needed it now.

***

VERY FEW THINGS targeted familiars—or perhaps I should say very few non-human things. And I'd never heard of anything that targeted wanna-bes, because a wanna-be's power, while considerable, wasn't really honed.

Wanna-bes were, for lack of a better term, the virgins of the familiar world.

And nothing targeted virgins (not even those stupid civilian terrorists. They got virgins as a *reward*).

So when I got out of the habitat, I had the computer search for strange creatures or things that targeted virgins. I got nothing.

Except the search engine, asking me a pointed electronic question:

Do you mean things that prefer *virgins?*

And I, on a frustrated whim, typed *yes*.

What I got was unicorns. Unicorns preferred virgins. In fact, unicorns would only appear to virgins. In fact, unicorns drew their magic from virgins.

But the magic was pure and sweet and hearts and flowers and Hello Kitty and anything else treacly that you could think of.

Except if the unicorn had become rabid.

I clicked on the link, found several scholarly articles on rabies in unicorns. Rabid unicorns were slightly crazed. But more than that, they had no powers because no virgin (no matter how stupid) was going to go near a horse-sized creature that shouted obscenities and foamed at the mouth.

That was stage one of the rabies. Unlike rabies in non-magical creatures, rabies in unicorns (and centaurs and minotaurs and any other magical animal) manifested in temporary insanity, followed by darkness and pure evil.

The craziness, in other words, went away, leaving nastiness in its wake.

Minotaurs, centaurs, and other such creatures attacked each other. They stole from the nearest mage—or enthralled him, stealing his magic before they killed him.

But unicorns…

Unicorns still needed virgins.

And the only solution was to steal the powers of wanna-be familiars.

Provided, of course, that the unicorn could find them.

And unicorns, like most other animals, hunted by scat.

***

I WISH I could say I got my giant unicorn-killing musket out of mothballs and carried it through an enchanted forest, hunting a brilliant yet evil unicorn that wanted to devour the untamed magic of wanna-be familiars.

I wish I could say I was the one who shot that unicorn with a bullet of pure silver and then got photographed with one foot on its side and the other on the ground, leaning on my musket like hunters of old.

I wish I could say I was the one who cut off its horn, then snapped the thing in half, watching the dark magic dissipate as if it never was.

But I can't.

Technically, I'm not allowed to leave the store.

So I had to call in the Homeland Security—Magical Branch anyway. I could have called the local mage police, but I wasn't sure where this unicorn was operating, and HS-MB had contacts worldwide.

They found four rabid unicorns all in the same forest, somewhere in Russia, along with a few rabid squirrels (probably the source of the infection) and a rabid magical faun that was going around murdering all the bears for sport.

The unicorns died along with the squirrels and that faun. The poop reappeared in my computer system, and went back through the normal channels. That week, we made double our money on magical fertilizer, which was good since we'd made none the week before.

All seemed right with the magical world.

Except one thing.

I dragged Fiona to her habitat so I could confront both her and Roy.

They usually didn't spend much time together. They blamed it on not really having a pride, but I knew the problem was Fiona. She hated having to hunt for him, then watch him eat the best parts.

She hated most things about feline life and once muttered, as yet another well adjusted young mage took a domestic cat as her familiar, that she wished she were small and cute and cuddly.

She had to fetch Roy. He wasn't going to come. He hadn't even attacked me as I entered the habitat—probably because Fiona was with me.

I waited as he climbed to the top of his rock, then assumed the same position he'd been in before he jumped at me. Only this time I was prepared. I had my sunglasses and my water bottle.

I also stood a few feet to the right of my previous position, a place he couldn't get to from the top of that rock.

Fiona sat at the base of the rock, beneath the outcropping, in the only stretch of shade in this part of the plain.

"You want to tell me how you did it?" I asked when Roy finally got comfortable. He sent me an annoyed look when he realized that I had stationed myself outside of his range. "You knew that there was a rabid unicorn after wanna-bes, and you somehow got the entire group at Familiar Faces to cooperate with you, all without leaving your habitat."

Then I looked at Fiona. She had left the habitat. She left it every single day.

The tip of her tail twitched, and she tilted her head ever so slightly, her eyes twinkling. But she said nothing.

Roy preened. He licked a paw, then wiped his face. Finally he looked at me, the hairs of his mane in place, looking as majestic as a lion should.

"I am king of the jungle," he said.

This is a plain, I wanted to point out, but I didn't for fear of silencing him. Instead I said, "Yet some of the other familiars don't live in habitats like yours. The snakes, for example."

He yawned. "The unicorn wasn't after them."

"But the animals?" I asked.

He closed his great mouth, then leaned his head downward, so that his gaze met mine. "The Russian Blues are refugees. You didn't know that, did you?"

I had two domestic cats—purebred Russian Blues. Most purebred cats aren't familiars—they have the magic bred out of them with all the other mixed genes—but these Blues were amazing. And pretty. And not that willing to talk, even when they knew it was the price of gaining a mage.

"Refugees?" I said. "They were adopted before?"

"Their mages murdered by the new secret police for being terrorists. I thought you checked all of this out."

I tried to, but I never could. Animal histories weren't always that easy to find.

"They'd heard rumors about something rabid getting into an enchanted forest somewhere in deepest darkest Russia. Then some young familiars—what you call wanna-bes—withered and died as their powers were sucked from them over a period of months."

He tilted his head, as if I could finish his thought.

And I could.

"So the Blues suspected unicorns," I said.

"There were always rumors of unicorns in that forest," he said, "but of course, none of us had ever seen them. For normal unicorns, you need virginal humans. None of us had encountered abnormal unicorns before."

I did the math. The Blues had arrived last Thursday, which was the last day Carmen had worked before Tuesday, when she discovered the problem.

"You went into protect mode immediately," I said.

"It is my pride, whether you admit it or not."

I didn't admit it, but I understood how he thought so. He needed a tribe to rule, so he invented one.

"I still don't understand what happened. You don't have the magic to make other animals' poop disappear."

"But they do," he said.

"I know that." I tried not to sound annoyed. He was toying with me again. I hated being a victim of cat playfulness.

"So how did you tell them what to do?"

He opened his mouth slightly, in that cat-grin of his. Then he got up, shook his mane, and walked back down the rock. He vanished in the tall grass, disappearing against its browness as if he had never been.

"He could tell me," I said.

"No, he can't." Fiona hadn't moved.

I let out a small sigh. He hadn't been toying with me. She had.

"You did it," I said.

"Me and the bees," she said. "They're creating quite a little communications network with those hive minds of theirs. They send little scouts into the other habitats every single time you go from one to the other. The ants too. You really should be more careful."

I felt a little frisson of worry. I had had no idea. I didn't want the bees to get delusions of grandeur. I already had to deal with Roy.

"You told them to spread the word."

She nodded.

"And you told them how the animals could hide their poop."

She inclined her head as regally—more regally—than Roy ever could.

"Why?" I asked. "You had no guarantee of a threat."

"This is the biggest gathering of the Hopeful on the globe," she said. "Of course we are a target."

She was right. I sighed, took a sip from my water bottle, and frowned. This entire event had opened my eyes to a lot of scary possibilities, things I had never considered.

We were going to have to rethink the way we handled waste. We were going to have to protect the poop somehow, and I didn't want to consult HS-MB about that. They'd have to hold hearings, and the wrong someone could be sitting in.

I didn't want us to become a magical terrorism target, nor did I want us to be a target for every rabid unicorn in the world.

I would have to set up the systems myself.

"You need me," Fiona said, "whether you like it or not. You can't have pretend familiars. You need a real one."

She was making a pitch. Cats never did that. Or they only did so if they believed something was important.

"Why here?" I asked. "I've found you some pretty spectacular possible mage partners, and you've turned them down."

She wrapped her tail around her paws and stared at me. For a moment, I thought she wasn't going to answer.

Then she said, "This is my pride. Roy might think it his, but he's a typical lion. He thinks he's in charge, when I do all the work."

She raised her chin. That tuft of hair that all lionesses had beneath looked more like a mane in the shade than it ever had. It made her look regal.

"Well," she added, "I'm not a typical lioness, content to hunt for her man and to feel happy when he fathers a litter of kittens on her only to run them out when they threaten his little kingdom. I don't want children. And I want to eat first."

"You can do that with other mages," I said.

"But I won't have a pride. Don't you see? I'm the one who spoke to the Blues. I'm the one who keeps track of those silly mice—even though I want to eat them—and I'm the one who calms the elephant whenever she has the vapors. No one credits me for it, of course, but it's time they should."

No one, meaning me. I hadn't noticed, and Fiona was bitter. Or maybe she just felt that I wasn't holding up my end of the bargain.

"Besides," she said, "it's hot in here. Can we go back to the air conditioning?"

I laughed and stepped out of the habitat. She followed.

"I'll petition the mage gods," I said.

"I already did." She was walking beside me as we headed toward the front room. "They said yes. I put their response under the cash register."

We went through the portal. The mice were having a party on top of the cheese books. One of the snakes was dancing too, trying to come out of its basket like a charmed snake from the movies. The dance was a bit pathetic, since the snake was the wrong kind. It was the tiniest of my garden snakes.

They all stopped when they saw me. I looked toward the mall's interior. The customer door was closed and locked and the main lights were off. The closed sign sat in the window.

Carmen had gone home long ago.

I went to the cash register and felt underneath it. Some dust, some old gum—and yes, a response from the mage gods, dated months ago.

"You took a long time to tell me this," I said to Fiona.

She wrapped herself around the counter. "You should clean more."

Come to think of it, a few months before was when she really started muttering her protests out loud. In English. She was doing everything felinely possible except blurting it out that she was now my familiar.

I had never heard of a familiar picking a mage.

Although that wasn't really true. The familiars always made their preferences known. I knew how to read the signs. For everyone, it seemed, but me.

"Do you regret this?" Fiona asked quietly.

"Hell, no," I said. "Your brilliance averted a major international incident and saved the lives of hundreds of familiars."

"Don't you think that makes me deserving of some salmon?"

I almost said *I think that makes you deserving of anything you damn well please,* and then I remembered that I was talking to a cat. A large, independent-minded, magical cat, but a cat all the same.

"Salmon it is," I said and snapped a finger. A plate appeared with the thickest, juiciest salmon steak I could conjure.

I set it down next to her.

"Next time," she said, "you're taking me out."

"Restaurants don't allow animals," I said. "At least, not in Chicago."

"I wasn't talking about a restaurant," she said. "I meant a salmon fishery or perhaps one of those spawning grounds in the wild. I heard there's a species of lion who hunts those grounds."

"Sea lions," I said. "You're not related."

She chuckled, then wrapped her tail around my legs, nearly knocking me over. Affection from my lioness.

From my familiar.

However I had expected my day to end, it hadn't been like this.

Carmen was right. This day had been weird.

But good.

"So are you going to promise to take me to a fishery after the next time I save lives?" Fiona asked.

"I suppose," I said, wondering what I had gotten myself into.

Fiona licked her lips and closed her eyes. The mice started dancing all over again, and chimpanzees came out of the back to see what the commotion was.

After a weird day, a normal night.

And I found, to my surprise, that I preferred normal to weird.

Maybe I was getting soft.

Maybe I was getting older.

Or maybe I had just realized that I was a mage with a familiar, a powerful smart familiar, one I could appreciate.

One who would keep me and my animals safe.

One who would rule her pride with efficiency and not a little playfulness.

I could live with that.

I had a hunch she could too.

Destiny

SOLANDA WALKED the cobblestone streets of Nir, the capitol city of Nye, her tail up. She had a meeting with Rugar, the son of the Black King. He had sent a Wisp to find her, and it had taken the little creature nearly a day to do so.

Solanda was in her cat form, as she had been since the Fey captured this repressed country — and thus very difficult to find. The Nyeians had many faults — they were prissy, overdressed, and pasty faced, not to mention abominably poor soldiers — but they did treat their animals well. She had found a family who fed her to excess, allowed her to roam outside, and pampered her as no cat should be pampered.

How appalled they would be if they ever discovered the golden cat their daughter had adopted was really a Fey Shapeshifter.

Solanda's tail twitched once in amusement. Every day she imagined eating her lovely tuna dinner in the glass plate that the family gave her, and then Shifting into her Fey form just to say thank you.

She didn't know what would appall the Nyeians the most: the fact that she was Fey, or the fact that she would be naked. She doubted any of them had seen a naked woman before: the wife managed to change her clothing one piece at a time, without ever taking it all off at once, and the husband didn't seem to think this unusual. He would probably be more shocked than his wife at the appearance of a naked Fey woman in his house. He would probably fall over in a dead faint.

Only the daughter, a girl of five, was redeemable. Esmerelda was a good child. She had to be. She was raised Nyeian. Her mother trussed her in layers upon frothy layers of clothing, making movement nearly impossible, and then yelled at the poor child whenever she did something natural, like running.

Sometimes Solanda thought she went back to that household at night because she felt sorry for the child. But in truth, she stayed there because they gave her fish properly deboned and they brushed her, and they put a warm cedar bed in Esmerelda's room. Esmerelda, good child that she was, never confessed to her parents that she often picked up the cat and carried her to bed, cuddling with her long into the night.

And Solanda would never tell anyone — Fey or Nyeian — that sometimes she purred when she slept, pressed against the little girl's back.

Shifters were supposed to be the coldest of the Fey, the most fickle members of a warrior people, incapable of real emotion, flighty, restless and completely self-absorbed. They also were supposed to take on the characteristics of the animal they had chosen to Shift into, so Solanda's fickleness — theoretically — was doubly compounded by the fact that she had chosen the cat as her alternate Shape.

Of course, it didn't matter how many times she had proven herself trustworthy. In the war against Nye, such as it was, she had done intelligence for the Black King. She had worn her cat form and slinked into Nyeian villages, soldiers' camps, and mess halls, keeping her ears open, and learning more than she should have.

Most countries that the Fey had fought had banned strange animals from military compounds. Solanda had heard that the Co had gone so far as to slaughter any strays, thinking they might be Fey reconnaissance. But the Nyeians had a fondness for cats, and while they kept stray dogs out of their camps, they fed cats on the side.

Solanda had spent most of the war the pampered resident of a Nyeian general's tent. He used to feed her bits of meat off his own plate while telling his staff his battle plans for the next day.

And then when he fell into his snoring sleep, she would go to the nearest Shadowlands and inform the Fey general of all she had heard. Toward the end of the war, she reported directly to the Black King, who shook his head at the stupidity of the Nyeians.

Conquering Nye was the first step toward world dominion. The Black King didn't say that, but Solanda knew that was his goal. The Fey were a great warrior people, but they only owned half the world right now. The Black King — and the Black Throne — wanted all of it.

Solanda entered the merchant sector of Nir, and silently cursed to herself. The merchants often shooed cats out of this area. Her presence here was suddenly noticeable, and she didn't dare Shift. She'd shock an entire community of Nyeians — which would probably be good for them.

Scents from the nearby vendor stalls caught her nose. Fried beef, more fish, some sort of vegetable something which turned her feline stomach. The fish was enticing. It almost made her forget that she was here because she had been summoned by the Black King's son.

Rugar had been her commander for part of the Nye campaign. He was an able warrior, frustrated under his father's tight leash. The problem with Rugar was that he believed himself to be the equal of his father, and he was not.

Solanda would rather work with the Black King, ruthless as he was, than with his less-talented son.

The tall stone buildings prevented the sun from getting to the cobblestone. The stone was wet beneath her paws from the morning rain. The air was thick and muggy, making the six layers of clothes the Nyeians wore look even more uncomfortable.

The handful of Fey who were on the street wore their traditional uniform — a leather jerkin and pants. The Fey were so much taller than the Nyeians that even if they didn't dress differently, they would be noticeable.

She ducked under some clothing stalls, past the buildings that housed the year-round indoor merchants, and turned on the street that led to the Bank of Nye. The Black King had taken over the building. It was four stories of gray stone, towering over the buildings around it — as close to a palace as there was in Nye.

She sighed heavily and crossed the street, climbing up the stone steps and staring at the large stone door. She'd have to Shift just to get into the place.

Then she saw a nearby window ledge. The window was open. She leaped onto the ledge and jumped to the stone floor inside. She thought this building unusually cold for a Nyeian structure. The house where she was pampered was made of wood, and had thick rugs on its floors. Every surface was soft, and the air perfumed.

Here the air smelled like chalk and the stone was chilly despite the heat. There were no guards in this room, although there should have been. It looked like it was someone's office — a desk in the center, chairs on the side for supplicants.

The door was open and led into a cavernous hallway. She heard voices and followed them. Several Fey guards huddled in an alcove. They were Infantry and young, tall even though they hadn't come into their magic yet. Their dark skin and black hair was a welcome sight. She'd gotten tired of looking at the pasty-faced Nyeians, and hadn't realized how much she missed her own kind.

"…fool's errand, don't you think?" One of the young men said.

"If it's so important, why doesn't the Black King go?" another asked.

"Blue Isle is important," said a young woman. "It's the only stop between here and Leut."

Leut was the continent on the other side of the Infrin Sea. The Black King wanted to go there more than anything. He wanted to conquer as much of the world as he could before he died.

"If we are going to conquer the world," the girl was saying, "we have to go through Blue Isle first."

"Then it doesn't make sense," the first man said. "Why send Rugar? He's not as good a commander as his father."

"Maybe," Solanda said in her most authoritative voice, "the best commander in the world has a plan that's too sophisticated for you to understand."

They all turned. They had similar upswept features, narrow faces, and pointed ears. Solanda had often thought that her people looked like foxes — most of them, anyway. Shifters, like her, often took some of the characteristics of their animals. Her hair and skin were more golden than dark, and she had the Shifter's mark on her chin — a birthmark that established who and what she was when she was in her Fey form.

But they couldn't tell now. All they could do was tell that a cat had spoken to them.

"Well," she said, sitting on her haunches and wrapping her tail around her paws. "Where do I start? Do I reprimand you for gossiping in the middle of the day?

Do I tell you that I got into the building through a window that some careless fool left open and, if I had been some young Nyeian bent on assassination, I could have walked right past you and you wouldn't have noticed? Or do I ask that one of you poor, magickless fools get me a robe so that I can have my meeting with Rugar?"

They didn't answer her. She raised her chin slightly. Amazing how she could intimidate them, even though she was so very small.

"By the Powers," she snapped. "Get me a robe. And put a guard on the window."

She nodded over her head toward the room she had just come out of.

Two of the young men ran off toward the room. The third young man hurried off, presumably to get her a robe. That left the young woman.

"I really should report this," Solanda said. "Technically, you put the Black King's life in danger."

"From the Nyeians?" the young woman snorted. "You snarl at them and they run. They couldn't fight us in the war, and once they found out that they'd remain in charge of their businesses, they really didn't care that we took them over. Why would one of them try to get in here?"

"Revenge?" Solanda said. "We did, after all, slaughter half their army. Those young men were related to someone."

"Then that should take away half the threat, shouldn't it?" the young woman said. "After all, the Nyeians believe that only men are capable of fighting."

Solanda felt amused. "I have a hunch that belief has changed since they were defeated by us. What's your name?"

"Licia," the girl said.

"You haven't come into your magic yet, have you?"

The girl straightened her shoulder. Magic was always a touchy subject with Infantry. They were tall enough to show that they would get magic, but chances were if they neared adulthood and still hadn't come into their magic, their abilities would be slight.

"No," she said.

"You showed a tactician's mind. Why do you waste it gossiping with people who aren't worthy of you?"

The girl straightened her shoulders. "I don't normally guard. I am usually in the field."

"But there's no field at the moment, is there?" Solanda said. "What are you doing here?"

"Rugar asked me to come. He says his daughter needs more swordfighting training."

Solanda narrowed her eyes. Jewel, Rugar's middle child, was the most promising of all his raggedy offspring. She hadn't come into her magic yet either, but her height and her heritage suggested when her magic came it would be powerful. She was a good swordswoman now — Solanda had seen her fight in the last of the Nye campaign.

"Why would she need more training?"

Licia shrugged. "I suspect it has something to do with the fight Rugar had with his father this morning."

Solanda tilted her head to show her interest.

"They just left that room you came through. They were screaming at each other all morning long."

"About what?" Solanda asked, realizing that she was now gossiping. But she didn't want to go into a meeting with Rugar with less knowledge than he had.

"About going to Blue Isle. Rugar says he won't go without his daughter."

"Not his other children?"

"He didn't mention them." Then Licia smiled. "At least not at the top of his voice."

Solanda suppressed a sigh. The Black King favored Jewel. He felt that her brothers were idiots — and he was right. Their magic was slight, like their mother's had been. Rugar's entire life had been about defying his father. Rugar should have married a woman who had great magic. Instead, he had chosen someone he could control.

The young man returned with a flowing golden robe that was clearly of Nyeian origin. Solanda didn't ask where he had gotten it. She didn't thank him. Instead, she said, "Place it over me."

He did, blotting out the light. The robe smelled faintly of perfume and perspiration, but it clearly hadn't been worn in some time. The fabric was heavy satin — too heavy for a humid day like this — but she wasn't in the position to be choosy. If Rugar was planning something stupid, she wanted to meet him Fey to Fey. Psychologically, it gave her an advantage.

She Shifted, feeling her body slide into its familiar Fey form. Her body stretched and grew. Her tail and whiskers slid into her skin, her hair flowed down her back, her front paws became hands. She ended up in a sitting position, her knees drawn to her chest, the robe draped over her like a tent. Inwardly she sighed, and wished that there were a more dignified way of Shifting into clothes.

Then she slid her arms through the sleeves, and her head through the neck hole, letting the stiff fabric flow around her. It was a woman's garment, although she had no idea why someone would store one in a bank — or perhaps she did, and didn't want to think about illicit affairs among Nyeian bankers.

She lifted her long hair out of the garment's neck, and let it fall down her back. Licia bit her lower lip, and the other Fey looked down. They hadn't realized they were talking to the best Shifter in the Black King's army — at least, not until now.

Fools. Shifters were rare. How many of them would come into the Black King's dwelling and order Infantry around?

"Licia," she said, "announce me to Rugar."

The girl's skin colored slightly, but she moved in front of Solanda and led her down the hall. It got stuffier the farther in they went. Solanda was grateful that her feet were bare. The cool stone was going to keep her from melting in this robe.

Licia led her up a flight of stairs into a rabbit's warren of what had once been offices. Solanda smiled. Rugar was hidden here, in an obviously less desirable area of the building. The Black King had a thousand ways of showing his displeasure with everyone around him.

Licia knocked on a door at the end of the hall. Solanda stood far enough back that she wasn't visible from inside. She heard Rugar's gruff voice, and then Licia's response, announcing Solanda.

The door opened, and Licia stepped aside.

"I guess that means you're supposed to go in," she said.

Solanda stopped and put a hand on the girl's shoulder. She spoke softly so that Rugar couldn't hear. "If Rugar and his father are fighting," she said, "side with the old man. Rugar is not the future of this race. You're better off remaining in Nye with the Black King than going to Blue Isle with Rugar."

Licia nodded, then glanced over her shoulder as if she were afraid of Rugar. Solanda walked past her and through the open door.

Rugar stood in the center of the small room. He was medium height for a Fey, and his features had a predatory, hawk-like look to them. His almond-shaped eyes were the deep black that Solanda associated with the Black Family. It was as if the Throne echoed in their very essence. He had thin cruel lips, and an expression of permanent unhappiness.

For man in his fifties with grown children, he looked startlingly like a petulant child.

"You sent for me," she said, not disguising her lack of respect for him.

He clasped his hands behind his back, his father's favorite stance. "I'm taking an army to Blue Isle. You will be part of it."

She snorted. "I serve your father, not you."

Rugar glared at her. "He gave me permission to choose whomever I wanted from the standing armies in Nye."

"You have no need for a Shifter," she said. "Blue Isle is a tiny place, filled with religious fanatics who have never seen war. You'll sail in with your troops, wave a few swords, and be able to claim victory over an entire country in the space of a day. I'll be useless to you."

He shook his head. "I'm taking you, and a lot of Spies and Doppelgängers. I am to be military governor of Blue Isle. My father will launch an attack from there onto Leut."

Solanda narrowed her eyes and was glad she wasn't in cat form. She probably would have found an excuse to scratch Rugar, and that wouldn't have been good for either of them.

"Spies, Doppelgängers, and a Shifter," she said. "It sounds like an intelligence force. You won't need it if you conquer the country as quickly as you believe you will."

His gaze went flat. "I will need it."

She stared at him for a moment. He knew something and he wasn't going to share it with her. Spies made sense, even in an easily conquered country. They would find the pockets of resistance. But Doppelgängers had no place there. They killed their hosts and then took over the body, including the memories. Except for the gold flecks in the eyes, no one could tell them from their victims. Doppelgängers had a sophisticated magic — one that the best commanders used sparingly. And certainly didn't waste them on an already conquered country.

"You have no need for me," she repeated. "I stay with the Black King."

"You'll come with me."

"Your father said so?"

"No, but he will."

"Because he already acquiesced on Jewel?"

Rugar started. He hadn't expected her to know that.

Solanda raised her eyebrows and allowed herself a small smile. "I am good at gathering intelligence."

"And," he said, "as you pointed out, there's no need for intelligence gathering in a conquered country."

She nodded. "I'll go to Leut with your father, when he's ready. Until then, I'll relax here."

"Solanda —"

"Rugar," she said, holding up a hand. "You and I have no great liking for each other. I have a hunch your father is sending you to Blue Isle to get you out of his sight. I'd rather not be associated with you in any way. Right now, I hold your father's respect. I'd rather not change that."

Rugar took a step toward her. She could feel the violence shimmering in him.

She grabbed the doorknob. "Touch me," she said, "and I'll scratch out your eyes."

"You can't touch me. I'm a member of the Black Family."

She smiled. "I'm a Shifter. Unpredictable, irresponsible, flighty — remember? I'm sure the Powers would let this slide."

"But my father would not," Rugar said.

"Oh," Solanda said softly, "but I think he would."

***

SHE TRIED TO SEE the Black King before she left the building, but he was nowhere to be found. His personal guards were gone as well. She decided she would find him in the morning, and went back to her life as a pampered Nyeian cat.

The home that she had chosen was a large one on the outskirts of Nir. It had two stories filled with more clutter than any home she had ever seen. Books of poetry, musical instruments, incredibly ugly paintings, and furniture everywhere. The only saving grace was that the furniture was comfortable and the kitchen had a cat door that she could escape through when the wife decided it was time for music.

Solanda slipped through the cat door, past the kitchen hearth. One of the three Nyeian servants was cleaning the pots from the evening meal. The air smelled faintly of roast beef, and Solanda's stomach rumbled.

Still, she didn't beg from the servant. She knew better. The idiot had kicked her "accidentally" once, and had the scars to prove it. But Solanda knew if she attacked anyone in the house too many times, she would be thrown out, and she wasn't willing to lose her rich dinners and soft bed just yet.

She blended into the hideous yellow wallpaper as she hurried up the stairs to Esmerelda's room.

Esmerelda sat on the edge of the bed, fingering a rip in her dress. She had a forlorn expression on her small face. Her brown hair hung limply around her cheeks, and a streak of dirt covered the pantaloons beneath the skirt.

Solanda had never seen Esmerelda look dirty before, nor had she seen the girl's hair loose at any time except bedtime.

"Oh, Goldie!" Esmerelda raised her voice in relief. She was speaking Nye, which was a language that Solanda hadn't known well when she moved into this house. Here her Nye had improved greatly, but she wanted to be fluent in it by the time she left.

The little girl launched herself off the bed and grabbed Solanda before Solanda could jump out of the way. Esmerelda wrapped her arms around Solanda and held tightly. Esmerelda had never done that before. If she had been a grabby little girl, Solanda would have been gone a long time ago.

So this meant, quite simply, that something was wrong.

Solanda let herself be held for a moment, then she turned her head toward the door and flattened her ears. Esmerelda, smart child that she was, understood both signals. She pushed the door closed, and then let Solanda go.

Solanda jumped on the windowsill. Esmerelda followed her, but didn't open the window like she usually did.

The room was hot and sticky. Solanda wouldn't be able to stay here too long if that window wasn't opened.

"I don't dare," Esmerelda said softly. "Mommy's really mad at me. She didn't even let me have dinner."

Now Solanda was interested, but she didn't want the story, not yet. She bumped her head against the window's bubbled glass.

Esmerelda bit her lower lip and shook her head.

Solanda placed a paw on the glass and meowed softly.

"Okay," Esmerelda whispered. "But if anyone comes, I'll have to close it."

Solanda almost nodded, then caught herself. When Esmerelda came close, Solanda bumped her affectionately with her head, and then watched as the little girl pulled the window open.

A cool breeze made its way inside. That was the other nice thing about this house. Esmerelda's room opened onto a large undeveloped area, so the smells of the outdoors came in strong. Breezes were unencumbered. Esmerelda's mother hated this, and often wished for close neighbors, but Solanda saw it for the blessing it was.

Esmerelda knelt down beside the window and put her elbows on the sill. She didn't touch Solanda, but she was still a bit too close. Her body heat was ruining the breeze.

"I been so bad," she said, "I won't get to go outside ever again."

Solanda watched her. The little girl had never been able to resist a cat's gaze. Solanda had never seen a child who was so very lonely. Esmerelda wasn't allowed to play — except with dolls whose clothing was frilly as the stuff she was trussed in — nor was she allowed to associate with the neighboring children who were, in her parents' mind, beneath her. She had lessons in poetry and music, art and dancing, but she liked none of it. What she really wanted to do was run as far as she could, and climb trees and learn how to swim.

She'd probably never get to achieve those goals.

"I was running this afternoon," Esmerelda said. Her face was wistful. She leaned her forehead against the glass. "Mommy was looking at fruit and I thought I could just go around the block, but she saw me. I guess she followed me."

Esmerelda had done this before, and it hadn't gotten her sent to bed with no supper. Solanda suspected the problem had something to do with the rip in the dress. Clothing was sacred, at least to this family. Solanda wanted to tear every piece so that this little girl could be free.

"She saw me fall." Esmerelda said, fingering her skirt. "She saw me hit a Fey."

Solanda stiffened. She almost asked who, and caught herself. Two near lapses in one conversation. She was getting much too relaxed with this child.

Esmerelda ran a soft hand over Solanda's head. Her touch was gentle again, as it had always been before.

"She said she was the Black King's granddaughter, and she yelled at Mommy for dressing me the way she did. And Mom yelled back. The lady said yelling at her was like yelling at all the Fey all at once."

Only one Fey woman could make that claim. Jewel. No wonder Esmerelda's mother was upset.

"And then Mommy told Daddy and he said that the Fey might hurt us. Because I ran." A tear coursed down Esmerelda's cheek.

And those fools were blaming the child for being a child. Solanda pushed against the girl's hand, and Esmerelda sniffled.

"I didn't mean to run. I just can't stay still sometimes."

Solanda understood that. She could never stay still. It was a curse of being a Shifter. It was the reason Fey wisdom said that Shifters were the most heartless of the Fey. Most Shifters did not have children, and most rarely stayed anywhere long enough to form a real relationship.

Esmerelda sighed. "I wish I was like you. I do what I want. Or like that Fey lady. She was nice to me. She didn't like Mommy though."

Neither did Solanda.

"She said children shouldn't be dressed like me. She said I ran into her because my clothing didn't let me run properly."

Probably true, Solanda thought.

"And that made Mommy really mad."

Esmerelda let her hand slide off Solanda's neck. She bunched her hands into fists and rested her chin on them, looking fierce and strong. Solanda felt her whiskers twitch in amusement. One day, Esmerelda's parents would no longer be able to control this child. If she was this strong, articulate, and intelligent at five, she would be impossible to control at fifteen.

Especially with all of the Fey influence around her.

"I wish I had magic," the little girl said. "Just a little bit. Then I could run and no one would know. I'd make myself invisible and no one would see me."

Solanda looked out the window, knowing her expression was too sympathetic for a cat. There was a ring of oaks at the edge of the lawn. They were blowing in the breeze. Maybe there would be another storm. Maybe this storm would finally cool the place off, although she doubted it. Nye's hot season was the worst she had encountered in any country she had ever been in.

"Esmerelda!" her mother's voice echoed from the hallway. "Why is your door closed?"

Esmerelda gasped and pulled down the window so quickly she almost caught Solanda's tail in it. Then she leaped onto the bed, stretching out. Solanda jumped beside her and curled up at her feet just as Esmerelda's mother opened the door.

The woman's face was flushed. She looked like a tomato about to burst. She was so tightly corseted that her body looked flat, and Solanda wondered how the woman could even breathe. She wore an evening dress of white satin that accented the redness of her face. The sides were lined with sweat.

"What are you doing?" she asked. Then she frowned. "How did that mangy cat get in here?"

Solanda growled softly in the back of her throat. She was not mangy. And the woman had never called her that before.

"I told you that you were supposed to be in here by yourself to think about what you did today. Things could have been much worse. Fortunately, she was in good mood. You know what those people can do? Why it's said they can cut the skin off a person with the flick of —"

Solanda yowled, and the woman stepped back, a hand over her heart. Esmerelda sat up, worry on her small face.

"Are you okay, Goldie?"

Solanda licked her right paw as if she had twisted it. She was not going to let that woman tell this little girl about Fey atrocities — even if they were true.

"Come on, Goldie," Esmerelda's mother said. "There's some beef for you in the kitchen."

Usually that would have gotten Solanda off the bed. But she could sneak down after everyone was asleep and take what she needed. Right now, she wanted to stay beside Esmerelda.

"Goldie," the woman said.

Esmerelda, good child that she was, bit her lower lip and said nothing. She didn't beg for the company that she obviously wanted.

"Goldie!" her mother sounded exasperated now. Then she shook her head. "Why do we put up with this animal?"

Neither Solanda nor Esmerelda answered.

Finally Esmerelda's mother sighed. "All right, she can stay. But I do expect you to sleep in that dress tonight and to think about how you could have hurt us all. That rip should be a reminder of the danger your misbehavior put us in. Nye isn't the place it used to be, child. Do something wrong, and those Fey will harm all of us."

Then she pulled the door closed, and Solanda heard the boards creak as she made her way down the stairs.

Esmerelda's fingers played with the rip. Solanda looked at it, then crossed the bed, took the skirt in her teeth and pulled. The rip grew. Esmerelda giggled, then covered her mouth. Solanda pulled harder. If the little girl had to sleep in these clothes, she might as well be comfortable.

Esmerelda ripped the pantaloons too, along the dirt line, giggling as she did so. "Mommy will think I did it when I was running," she said. "You're so smart, Goldie."

Of course she was. Solanda preened and allowed herself to be petted one more time.

Then Esmerelda looked at the door, her smile fading. "Sometimes I think Mommy doesn't want me. She wants somebody else. Somebody perfect."

Too bad she didn't realize that the child she had was better than perfect. Solanda sighed softly. Some people had more than they deserved.

***

THE IDEA CAME to her in the middle of the night, in that hot and stuffy room. She could take Esmerelda away, and Esmerelda's parents wouldn't even know it had happened. But it would take the cooperation of the Fey Domestics.

Fey magic was divided into two parts: warrior and domestic. Warrior magic was designed for warfare. Some Fey magic turned its practitioner into a weapon, like the Foot Soldiers who had fingernails that could slice better than a blade. Domestic magic could not be used to fight any war. Domestics lost their magic if they killed. Their magics were healing magics or home-bound magics, such as spells that made chairs more inviting or fires warmer.

The next morning, after making certain that Esmerelda got breakfast, Solanda slipped out the cat door. She went to the Domicile that the Fey Domestics had set up just outside of town. The Domicile had been built especially for the Domestics, and covered with various protection and healing spells. It was a traditional U-shaped building — with hearth and home magics in one length of the U, the healing wards in the other, and the middle section as a meeting place in between.

Solanda usually didn't seek out the Domestics. They always wanted to experiment with her — have her try on a new cloak covered with some sort of rain protection or have her taste a new food to see if it had an effect on her Shifting. The last time she had been in a Domicile had been when she had broken a paw jumping from a tree in one of the last Nye battles. The Domestics had mended the bone, and had given her a smelly ointment she had to apply in cat form. She had thought the stench alone would kill her.

As she mounted the steps to the center part of the building, she shook off her paws. Here she would not Shift to Fey form. The Domestics weren't as obsessed with power as Rugar was, so she didn't have to use her height as a reminder of the strength of her magic.

She pushed open the door and stepped inside.

The air was cool and welcoming. It smelled of a sea breeze. Bits of magic floated in the air. Spinner's magic. They were working on their looms. She could hear the hum just down the corridor.

A Baker entered, his fingers dusted with flour. They glowed. And she knew he had spelled the bread he'd been baking to remain fresh for as long as possible. It was a traveling spell, one most often used when troops were heading off to battle. She wondered if someone had requested it.

"I'm here to see Chadn."

The Baker nodded, then slipped through a door that led to the Healing part of the Domicile. Solanda hopped onto a chair. Her mood rose and she cursed, jumping down. She didn't need to be spelled, to wait, happy and contented, on a chair dusted with Domestic magic. Instead she paced the cool floor and wondered why she couldn't smell the baking bread.

Finally Chadn entered the room. She was a young Shaman, although the toll of her power had already turned her hair white. Her face was wizened, her mouth

a small oval amid wrinkles. Only her eyes were bright —
sparkling black circles of light in a ruined face.

She had been assigned to stay with Rugar during
the war and she was happy to be free of him. Shaman
were the most independent Fey: their Vision as strong
as those of the Leaders, but their magic Domestic so
they could not rule a warrior people. They were the wise
ones, the advisors, supposedly the strength behind the
Black Throne. The Black King required a Shaman of his
son, but did not use one himself. He had dismissed his
own, years ago, for disobeying him. It was one of many
areas where the Black King broke with tradition.

"Solanda," Chadn said. "I had hoped to see you."

Solanda jumped on an end table and was relieved
that her mood did not change. She sat on her haunches
and looked into Chadn's face.

"I have a request," she said. "It's for a Nyeian child."

"A child?" Chadn sounded surprised. "Not a Fey child?"

Solanda shook her head.

"I had Seen you with a Fey child."

The Shaman's Visions — and the Vision that leaders like the Black King had — allowed them glimpses
into the future. Some said that the glimpses allowed the
Visionary to change the future. Others believed that the
glimpses led the Visionary to that future.

Solanda's eyes narrowed. "I have not been with a Fey
child."

Chadn nodded. "It was on Blue Isle. The child was a
Shifter, and you kept her from death."

Solanda's whiskers twitched. "I told Rugar I would not go to Blue Isle with him."

"The future of our people lies with you, Solanda."

"And a child?" Solanda raised her chin. "Are you sure it was a Fey child?"

"Not entirely," Chadn said. "The child had blue eyes."

Solanda gave a soft grunt of surprise. She had heard of blue-eyed people, but she had never seen one. "The child couldn't be Nyeian?"

"She was Fey, and newborn. She had a birthmark on her chin. Only her eyes were strange, and perhaps that was because of the Shifting. I Saw you put your hands on her lips, and swear to protect her, raise her, and make her strong. Then I Saw her full grown, saying you had been the closest thing she had to a mother."

Solanda laughed, although inside she felt cold. A Shifter only swore to protect a child who held the future of the Empire. A blue-eyed child that Shifted? The center of the Empire?

"Visions can be altered," Solanda said. "I am not leaving Nye."

"You may have no choice."

"I'll always have a choice," Solanda said.

Chadn inclined her head toward Solanda as if giving in on that point. "What does the Nyeian child need?"

Solanda took a deep breath. "She is different from any other Nyeian I've seen. Strong, independent. She met Jewel yesterday and is being punished for it. I would like to remove the child from her family and bring her here, to be raised among us. She will be useful when she's grown. She will be part of the second-generation, the Nyeians that rule Nye for the Fey."

Chadn stared at her for a moment. "So take her. Shifters steal children."

"This one's mother will raise a fuss if she's gone."

"What mother wouldn't?"

"She'll come to us."

"And you can't prove to the Black King that we must keep the child."

"Not yet, anyway," Solanda said.

Chadn folded her hands over her stomach. "You want a Changeling."

"Yes," Solanda said.

"How old is the child?"

"Five."

Chadn sighed. "Have you asked the child if she's willing to leave?"

"Not yet. I wanted to know if I have help first."

"You will keep the child at your side?"

Solanda frowned. That wasn't a normal request. Shifters rarely kept children. They usually brought them to Domestics to raise. "Must I?"

"At five, it will be you she trusts."

Solanda shrugged. "Then she shall stay with me."

"And you will stay away from Blue Isle." Chadn said that not as a question, but as a statement.

"Rugar will not let a Nyeian child in his war party."

"So the child serves two purposes." Chadn's eyes narrowed. "Has she magic?"

"Of course not." Solanda laughed. "There is not magic outside the Fey."

Chadn frowned. "I am no longer certain of that."

"Because you Saw a blue-eyed Shifter?"

"Because I Saw a great war, coming when we least expect it."

"War is part of Fey life." Solanda jumped off the table and headed for the door. "I'll bring you news of the child tomorrow."

"I'll have Changeling stone ready," Chadn said. "But realize before you act, that this is for life."

"I already know that," Solanda said. "I have chosen well."

"I hope so," Chadn said.

***

Solanda went to the docks and sat on a fence. She loved it here. The Infrin Sea formed the most natural harbor on Galinas, and there was always some sort of activity. Toward the north end of the harbor, the Nyeian builders made the great ships. Those ships traveled all over the known world, and now Fey Domestics helped unload cargo that would go all over the Empire.

Ships from Blue Isle had stopped coming to Nye when news reached them of the Fey takeover. She would never see an Islander, never learn more about them than she already had.

And that would be all right.

For there were some things she couldn't discuss with Rugar's Shaman. Like the prophecies that had been made by another Shaman at Solanda's birth, prophecies that claimed her legacy would be in the children she saved.

Children — not child, like Chadn had seen. Solanda would influence the life of more than one.

The breeze was cooler here, carrying with it the smell of salt and a tinge of dead fish. That smell made her stomach rumble. She tried not to think of the things she ate in her cat form, things she would find disgusting when she was in Fey form. Right now, raw dead fish sounded extremely appetizing.

But she didn't go in search of the source of the smell. She had some thinking to do. Prophecies and Visions made her nervous. She had no idea what to do with the information Chadn had given her. Because, at various points in her life, Solanda had been told by Visionaries that her future held contradictory things.

One Shaman had told her she had to avoid the Black Family for she would kill a Black Heir. Another Shaman had told her she would raise a Black Heir. And now Chadn had Seen her swear to protect a blue-eyed Shifter, a newborn who couldn't survive on her own.

Solanda bowed her head. The prophecy she never mentioned, the one her parents had kept silent, had come the day of her birth and she had never forgotten it. The prophecy was a cold one: she would die before her time, far from home, for a crime she did not regret.

The Fey did not believe in crime. They were constantly at war, so the crimes that plagued other races — murder, theft — were absorbed into the wars themselves. The Fey only punished two crimes: treason and failure. Both of those crimes were considered crimes against the Empire. Failure was a large crime, encompassing the failure to follow an order, or the failure to defeat an enemy in a prolonged battle.

Treason was any crime against the Black Family and was such a heresy, that it wasn't even discussed among rational Fey.

Both crimes bore the penalty of death.

It seemed to her that she would never commit crimes like that, that the prophecies had come because she was a Shifter, not because of her character. She wasn't as flighty or as difficult as anyone said she was.

And besides, she had to take care of Esmerelda.

She wished she could be there the morning that Esmerelda's parents discovered the Changeling. It would look like Esmerelda, even act like her — if stone could act like a living breathing creature. But it would only last a few days, and then it would cease to exist. They would think Esmerelda dead, when, in actuality, she was only gone.

Then, perhaps, that wretch of a mother would regret how she treated her daughter.

Esmerelda would live a life she couldn't even imagine now. She wouldn't have to wear six layers of clothes on the hottest day of the year, and she would learn how to live life to its fullest instead of remaining indoors and studying all the time.

Esmerelda would be the closest thing to Fey that a Nyeian could be — and for the first time in her young life, she would be happy. Solanda would see to that.

They would both be very happy.

***

SOLANDA RETURNED to the house after dinner. Ultimately, she found she couldn't resist the dead fish that were piled near one of the docks. She had eaten herself sick, and then had to clean every inch of her fur before she even attempted the walk home.

Not that the house was home. In some ways, Esmerelda was.

Solanda used the cat door. Esmerelda's parents were talking softly in the parlor.

"Perhaps boarding school," the mother was saying. "If she is this incorrigible now, imagine what she'll be like when she gets older."

"Give it time, darling," the husband said. "She's still a child. She will learn, as we all did."

"It's just I despair of ever teaching her manners. You didn't see her with that Fey…."

Solanda had heard enough. She hurried up the stairs. She would talk to Esmerelda tonight. Tomorrow the Wisps would come, carrying a bit of stone in their tiny fingers. They'd fly in the open window, leave the stone on the bed and it would mold itself into a replica of Esmerelda while Solanda was leading the real Esmerelda out of the house.

Quick, neat, and completely perfect. The parents wouldn't have to worry about manners or boarding school. Esmerelda would get her heart's desire. And Solanda would have her reason for staying in Nye.

The door to Esmerelda's room was open. Esmerelda sat beneath a lamp, a long skirt over her lap. The air was stuffier than usual, and Solanda saw that the window was closed.

It had probably been closed all day. Sunlight had poured in, and the poor child had had to sit in the heat, working on some task her mother assigned her.

When Solanda got close, she saw what it was. The child was attempting to mend her own ripped dress.

The stitches were uneven, and Esmerelda had stitched the bottom layer of fabric onto the top. That would make her mother even angrier. Esmerelda's eyelashes were stuck together, her nose was red, and there were tearstains along her cheeks.

"Goldie!" she said, and let the dress topple to the floor. She was wearing another dress, equally inappropriate to the hot weather. She reached for Solanda, but Solanda jumped onto the windowsill.

She was not going to be hugged by a hot sweaty child — not, at least, until the window was open and the fresh air came inside.

Esmerelda glanced toward the door. She put a finger to her lips, as if she thought Solanda were going to give her away, and then called, "Mommy! Can I go to sleep now?"

Solanda froze in her spot. She didn't want to be seen in here, not tonight. She wanted to have her conversation with Esmerelda in private.

"Are you done with your dress, darling?"

"Yes."

Solanda looked at it. The dress was ruined. The poor girl would have an even more difficult day than usual tomorrow.

"Then blow out the lamp. Good night."

"Good night." Esmerelda pushed the door closed. Then she went over to the window and opened it.

A strong breeze came in, and on it, Solanda smelled rain. Maybe, after she spoke to Esmerelda, she would go outside. By then it would be raining, and she would be able to cool down.

Esmerelda put her hand over the lamp's chimney and blew. The flame inside the glass went out. Solanda blinked in the darkness, letting her eyes adjust. It only took a moment. There were clouds over the moon this night, and it was very dark.

Esmerelda went back to her chair. "I wish you knew how to sew, Goldie."

"I don't," Solanda said. "But I know someone who does."

Esmerelda let out a small yelp, and put her hands over her mouth. She peered around the room as if looking for the source of the voice.

Solanda had to go slowly with this. The child wasn't used to magic, not like Fey children were.

"I could take the dress to her tonight," Solanda said, "and by morning, you wouldn't even know there had been a rip in it."

Esmerelda's eyes were wide. She finally turned in Solanda's direction. "You can talk, Goldie?"

"As well as I can listen." Solanda jumped from the windowsill to the bed. The room had cooled down. The fresh air felt marvelous. "What would you think, Esmerelda, if I took you to a place where you could wear comfortable clothes, play with children your own age, run and jump and swim to your heart's content? What if I told you that you would never have to sew another stitch, have another music lesson, or sit in a corner when you've done something that your mother didn't like."

Esmerelda looked for her, but clearly didn't see her. Cat's eyes were far superior in the dark. Solanda watched the child lick her lips, rub her hand over her knees, and then sigh.

"How long would I stay?" Esmerelda asked.

"Forever," Solanda said.

"Would I have to be a cat?"

Solanda laughed. For all her verbal sophistication, Esmerelda was still a child at heart. "No," Solanda said. "You'll stay just as you are."

"Would Mommy come?"

"No."

"Daddy?"

"No."

Esmerelda's shoulders stiffened. Her little body looked rigid. "Who would love me then?"

Solanda started. She hadn't expected that question. "I would be with you," she said.

Esmerelda was silent, as if she were thinking this over. "Where would you take me?"

"To my people," Solanda said.

"I'd live with cats?"

"No," she said gently. "With the Fey."

Esmerelda gasped. She held onto her chair as if she expected to be dragged from it.

Solanda wondered if she should have said that, but she had never taken a child before. Certainly she knew of no one who had ever taken a child of this age.

But Chadn had said she had had to speak with the child, and the choice to come had to be the child's. There was sense in that. Esmerelda, at age five, would always have a memory of living with her parents. She needed a memory of her choice to leave them.

"Esmerelda," Solanda said. "I—"

"No!" Esmerelda screamed. "No!"

She launched herself out of her chair as if her voice had given the ability to move again.

"Help! Mommy! Help!"

Solanda's ears went back. She hadn't expected this from Esmerelda, not her sane, different child.

"Esmerelda, I only want to give you a better life—"

"Mommy! Daddy! Help!"

Finally Esmerelda pulled the door open and blundered into the hallway. Solanda followed, tail between her legs, ears still back. The little girl's screams echoed down the stairs. Her parents had reached her, and they both put their arms around her. Esmerelda was too terrified to be coherent.

Then the mother looked up the stairs. She saw Solanda, her gaze flat.

And Solanda realized she had no choice.

She Shifted, her body lengthening, her tail disappearing, her fur becoming skin.

Then she walked, naked, to the floor below.

Esmerelda's mother gathered her child in her arms and backed away. The father placed himself in front of his small family, arms out.

"You came from the Black King, didn't you?" the woman said. "To punish us by stealing our child."

"It's not about you," Solanda said.

Esmerelda peeked around her father, eyes wide. Solanda had never, in her entire life, been so conscious of her nakedness.

"Wh-what do you want?" the father asked. He was trying to sound brave. Like most Nyeians, he was failing.

"I had hoped to take your daughter, but it seems that she prefers this place, even though you treat her as less than house pet. It seems, for reasons I cannot understand, that she loves you."

"Of course she does," the woman said. "We're her parents."

"As if that's a divine right." Solanda stopped on the middle stair.

The family cringed below her as if they expected her to strike them with a lightning bolt. She didn't have that kind of magic. They had seen the extent of her powers, but apparently they didn't know that.

"She is a child," Solanda said. "She is to run and play. She is to have friends of her own age. She is to have comfortable clothing so that she can move without tripping. She is supposed to get dirty, to rip her skirts, and fall on her behind. She is to have some joy in her life. Do you understand?"

"I thought you Fey were supposed to leave us alone," the mother said. "I thought —"

"Be quiet," the father said.

Esmerelda clung to her father, her curiosity moving her closer.

"You will give her those things," Solanda said, "or I will take her from you. Do you understand?"

"Yes," the father said.

"You can't do this," the mother said. "You can't change our customs. The Black King promised you wouldn't."

"A promise made to a conquered people is worth nothing," Solanda snapped. "You will do what I say, or the child is mine."

"Mommy." Esmerelda reached for her mother. Solanda's eyes narrowed. Couldn't she see that her mother saw her only as a thing to be trained, to be forced into the right and proper life?

Probably not. It was too sophisticated a concept for her. The same innocence that allowed Esmerelda to accept a cat's speech, allowed her to believe that she was loved.

"Do I take her now?" Solanda asked.

"No," the father said. "We'll do as you say."

"But our friends —"

"Shut up," the father snapped. "Do you want to lose her?"

For a moment, the mother's gaze met Solanda's and in it, Solanda saw something she recognized, a coolness perhaps, a calculation. How would that woman have answered if she had been asked *who would love me then?* Would she have dodged the answer like Solanda had? Or would she have heard it at all?

"She will stay with us," the woman said. She sounded resigned.

Solanda felt a hope she hadn't even known she had die inside her. "Then I'll watch. You will treat that child as if she is more precious than gold. And if you fail, even once, she's mine. Is that clear?"

"Yes," the father said.

But Solanda did not take her gaze from the mother.

"Yes," the woman said.

Esmerelda had stepped to her father's side. She was still holding his leg. "Are you Goldie?" she asked.

Solanda gave her a small, private smile. "Only for you."

The little girl slipped behind her father again. Her answer was clear, too. She would stay, no matter what. And Solanda had done all she could.

So she Shifted back to her cat form. For a moment, she watched them all, tail twitching, then she ran up the stairs and into Esmerelda's room. She stopped for only a moment, knowing she would never return.

She leapt onto the windowsill, and sighed. She had just lost her excuse for staying on Nye. She was bound to the Black Family. She had to do as they wished.

Rugar wanted her to go to Blue Isle.

Where a Shifter awaited her care. A newborn child, with blue eyes. A child who would think her the closest thing she'd ever had to a mother.

Solanda looked over her shoulder. She heard Esmerelda's voice, high, piping, excited; the soft answers of her parents. Solanda had lied to them. She would not be able to watch.

She hoped they would take good care of her little girl.

Then she jumped out the window, and climbed along a tree branch. Maybe her future had been preordained. Maybe she had no choice. She would raise a Black Heir, maybe kill one, and influence children.

How different would tonight have been if she had told the child that she would love her?

She would never know. Perhaps that was the moment in which everything could have changed. Maybe she had just missed her only chance to save herself.

About the Author

INTERNATIONAL BESTSELLING WRITER Kristine Kathryn Rusch has published dozens of novels, including seven books about the Fey. Published all over the world, the Fey novels have recently been rereleased in the United States as audio books by Audible.com. In addition to many awards in the science fiction and fantasy fields, she has been nominated for three Edgar Awards, two Shamus Awards, and an Anthony Award. She has won the Ellery Queen Reader's Choice Award twice, once for "The Secret Lives of Cats." For more information about her work, go to kristinekathrynrusch.com.